PREPARE

TO MEET

THY GOD

PREPARE

TO MEET

THY GOD

Matt Starr

A
Grinning Skull Press
Publication

ISBN-13: 978-1-947227-54-5 (paperback)
ISBN: 978-1-947227-55-2 (e-book)

DEDICATION

To friends. The kind that take you in, no matter how weird or messy you are. The kind that pick you and keep you moving.

ACKNOWLEDGMENTS

I never thought I'd be here. My work has certainly had dark leanings in the past, but if you told me I'd be publishing a supernatural Appalachian gothic with monsters, blood, guts, and drugs, I might have been hard pressed to believe you. I'm glad I surprised myself. I owe, first and foremost, a great deal of inspiration to the campy scary flicks of the 70s and 80s; to literary horror and dystopian masters like Ballingrud, Barker, Butler, and King; to gothic giants like Jackson and McCarthy.

80 percent of this book was written in the break-room at the offices of my employer, Reunion Marketing, so I'd be remiss to not acknowledge them. To anyone who saw me typing my lunch away like I'd die if I stopped: now you know. So many people played a role in this project—which afforded me the most fun I've ever had writing—but none so much as my friends. You know who you are.

I'd like to say thank you to my dogs, who give me purpose and silently judge me with healthy doses of side-eye on a daily basis. Thank you to my number one fan, my mama. Thank you to my family on all sides, who act like I'm bound for a bestseller list every time I announce the smallest short story acceptance—even when the work is a little too strange and intense for their taste. Thank you to my proofreader and biggest supporter, Emily. You make it all worth it.

Grinning Skull Press took a lot of care with this thing, and for that, I'm endlessly grateful. And, of course, you. From the bottom of my heart, thank *you* for reading.

Watch ye therefore: for ye not know when the master of the house cometh.

–Mark 13:35

Part 1

Chapter One

I didn't think a weekend getaway to the mountains with my girlfriend's friends seemed like all that bad of an idea. It would have to beat the hell out of a sweltering, sticky, and mosquito-plagued summer camping trip to the lake, all of us dehydrated and stinking and sore from sleeping on the ground. There was no way it would be any worse than waking up at spring break in Myrtle Beach, breath thick with cigarettes, beer, and dumb words that nobody remembers.

That's what I thought before more than half of us were dead.

We'd all been at the bar shortly after Thanksgiving, and someone, as you often do when you're shitfaced, proposed grand plans—the type that you don't typically follow through with but sound pretty damn good at the time. "We should all go on a skiing trip to the mountains," Beau said. "After New Year's. Martin Luther King weekend or somethin."

Beau was the emotional dad of the group, though he was also one of the youngest: a life-sized teddy bear of a man with sleepy eyes and an easy smile. We all knew that our time and money would be depleted after the holiday season, but Beau had this effortless ability to make things sound like they made all the sense in the world.

"A big group of us," he said. "Just a couple of days. That way, it'll be cheap."

We all agreed—or at least acquiesced—some of us in a more altered state of mind than others. It's hard to say no to most anything at last call. I didn't think much of it for a few weeks after that, but then Willa sent me a text with the link to a rental property everybody was looking at on the HomeAway app. The two-story house was on three hundred acres of land in southeastern West Virginia, a forty-five-minute drive from the Virginia state line and a four-hour road trip from our little townhouse in suburban Durham, North Carolina. It looked like an adequate space for a weekend of drinking, drugs, and belligerent behavior. There was a wraparound porch, a recreation area in the basement, a living room, and six bedrooms—three upstairs, three downstairs—as well as sofas and futons to crash on.

But I was skeptical nonetheless. The trip was going to cost at least a hundred dollars I didn't have, and at the end of the day, the people going were Willa's friends, not mine. The truth is, I didn't have any friends of my own, and even though I'd warmed up to hers since we'd started dating a year and a half before, I still didn't feel like part of the group. Not entirely. I'm sure a lot of it had to do with them being recent college grads and me being a hair shy of thirty years old. I'd had my share of moments with them, but there was still a distance that I couldn't quite put my finger on.

Still, it had been an unseasonably warm winter at home, and the forecast north of us called for lows in the teens. The mountains had always been a place of serenity for me, and I reckoned the cold, tranquil landscape would do me some good. And so it was that when the Friday nine-to-five came and went on the second to last full week of January, I left work, picked out a fifteen-dollar cigar, a nice-ish bottle of wine, and a couple of sixers of beer, and headed for our townhouse, hoping for the best.

Chapter Two

I could hear the patter of Pinto's paws on the hardwood floors from the porch. I opened the door, and our beagle-dachshund mix stretched so hard he could barely keep his footing. He jumped, only once, then retreated into the living room, waiting for me to take my place on the couch. I obliged, and he plopped down on the floor next to me, his bean-shaped body grazing my ankle. My little buddy.

"Good boy, Pinto," I said, fishing for the phone in my jacket pocket. I googled Blue Brier, which was the town we'd have to go through to get to the house, and my search yielded few results. One of them, at least, looked like the town's official website. It had an archaic layout and took forever to load, but when it did, the words "Almost Heaven" popped up in the header. I had a good laugh at that because those words didn't reflect my experience with West Virginia at all. I'd only been there a few times to visit a friend's grandparents, but most of the areas I'd encountered were heavily impoverished and outdated. Looking at the pixelated photos on Blue Brier's website, I didn't have much to convince me otherwise. But I also realized that I probably wasn't being fair.

I started to scroll down when a car horn sounded in the parking lot outside. Pinto yowled and tore off toward the door. Seconds later, Willa entered the townhouse, arms full of grad school books and a tote bag from work. She dropped everything to hug Pinto, who jumped not once or twice, but six or seven times, and I got as jealous as I always did. Pinto was my dog, but Willa was his human.

She rounded the corner. "Hey, baby," she said.

I gave her a good look over. She had been named Willow, but her very Southern grandmother pronounced the second syllable with an "a," and I guess it caught on. She was short, but her heart was big. She was bright, but her eyes were a deep brown. She was quiet, but her smile was loud. I loved her quite a bit.

"Hey," I replied, giving her a hug and a kiss.

Pinto interjected with a woof.

"You packed up?" she asked.

"Pretty much," I said. "When are Mike and Maggie getting here?"

"Soon, I hope. All the couples are gonna get there before us and claim the beds." She laughed nervously. She was anxious like that. "A few people are already there."

"Who?" I asked.

"Beau and Delco, I think. Maybe a few others."

"Delco?" I asked. "Goddammit."

"Heath," Willa said.

Nobody knew what Delco's real name was. He was a transplant from Delaware County, Pennsylvania, and I didn't like him. Everyone else in the friend group did, though—even Beau, and he hated Yankees. Delco was the life of the party and everybody's pal, but I didn't trust him, and I'd always considered myself a pretty good judge of character.

"I just don't understand why he shows up to everything," I said.

"Because he's part of the group. We met him sophomore year, and technically everyone's known him for longer than they've known you."

I went over to the kitchen table and rearranged some of the items in my bookbag, trying to act like what she'd said didn't sting as much as it did.

"You just don't like him because he hit on me that one time."

If there was any truth in that, I wasn't going to acknowledge it. "Well, if he gets out of line and starts hitting walls and shit like he normally does when he's drunk, I'll put him in his place."

"Okay," she said, rolling her eyes.

The doorbell rang, and a patchy-faced, messy-haired guy wearing a gray hoodie pushed into the townhouse. Or maybe the hoodie was wearing him. He nodded at us and said hello to Pinto like he was a person.

"What was the point of ringing the doorbell if you were just gonna come in anyway?" Willa asked him.

"I didn't wanna be rude," Mike said.

Willa rolled her eyes for the second time in as many minutes. "Where's Maggie?" she asked.

"She's right behind me."

"Oh good," Willa said. "Let's go load up the car."

I opened the door, and Maggie stood there on the porch, a jumbled mess of curly red hair and more bags than anyone could possibly need for the weekend. She cut her eyes past me. "Thanks for holding the door for me, Mike."

"You're welcome," he said. Mike and Maggie weren't together, but they squabbled like an old married couple. They couldn't have been much more different from each other than they already were. He was an even-tempered stoner with a predilection toward cheesy jokes. She was a livewire splayed across the street in the aftermath of a storm.

"Shall we?" I said.

We walked out to Willa's SUV, a new, pearly white crossover she'd just traded her starter car for. And she was proud of it. "Y'all, please be careful when you're putting stuff in," she said. "Lift up, don't drag." She made gestures with her hands like a flight attendant explaining how to activate a flotation device.

I shook my head. "Sooner or later, you're gonna have to lighten up," I warned her, opening the backleft door. I put Pinto's harness on and buckled him in. He responded in typical dramatic fashion.

Mike retrieved his suitcase from his car, and we stacked the hatch of Willa's SUV from floor to roof. As Maggie situated her four bags in the heap, I stepped away. I sized up a capsule in my palm and threw it back without water. There was the slightest head rush as it traced my digestive tract.

"Your medicine?" Willa asked.

I nodded. In a way, I guess it was.

We belted in, and I fired up the engine. Our first stop would be Yadkinville, one hundred miles or so away. Willa's parents had agreed to babysit Pinto for the weekend, and we'd meet them there. The blue hour of the day had just commenced, and we had a long drive ahead of us. Our destination was "Almost Heaven," but the same hellish apprehension I'd wrestled with for most of my life began to hollow itself into my bones. I didn't kick up too much piss about it. How could I? It had been there for as long as I could remember.

Chapter Three

My girlfriend thought I never wanted to hang out with her friends because I was too old and looked down on them as childish and inexperienced. But that wasn't the case. It's true that I sometimes observed their shenanigans through the lens of been-there-done-that, but it was much deeper. I had lost something at their age that I knew I'd never get back. And I was jealous of them because they hadn't.

I was raised by a single mother who busted her ass to make sure I had clothes on my back and food in my stomach. Sometimes the clothes were from a thrift store, and most times, the food was prepared by Stouffer's, but we did the best with what we had. She dragged me along with her to the dentist's office she worked at because she couldn't afford a babysitter. She helped me with my homework every night of the week, even if it meant she had to learn the material herself. If she took a lunch break at all, it was to attend an honor roll that I couldn't have made without her. She cooked and cleaned when she had the time. She mowed

13

the yard.

She was so proud of me when I got into college. But I made it all of three semesters before a lifestyle of partying and the stress of being on my own caught up to me. The transition to college is a pretty big adjustment for anybody, but the growing pains were tenfold for me. I drank and smoked whatever I could get my hands on. Blacked out so many times that there are gaps in my memory that even the most damned ghosts won't haunt. Then one day on a comedown, the emotional toll became too difficult to bear.

I remember that call well:

"Hey, Mama," I'd said.

"Hey, Darlin," she'd replied in her Southern voice—the voice of a woman who'd been brought up in a vernacular house in segregated North Carolina—undoubtedly dropping whatever she was doing to give me every bit of her attention. "What're you doin?"

"Nothing much." I was trying not to cry. I'd been told all my life that men didn't cry. "I'm thinking about coming home."

"For the weekend?"

"No. For good."

There had been a pause. "You ain't thinkin about droppin out, are you?"

"I don't know what I'm thinking about," I'd said. "I just don't feel good."

"What do you mean you don't feel good?"

"I don't feel like I belong. I feel like I'm wasting my time." I'd rarely gotten sick as a child, and when I did, it was serious, so I know she believed me when I said I wasn't well. It wasn't physical this time, but it was no less debilitating.

"All right," she'd said. "Well, you know you can always come home. But I sent you off to school to have a good life."

"I know."

"And I want you to promise me, right here and now," she'd continued, "that if you do this, you'll go back and finish."

"I promise," I'd said. I hadn't meant it, though.

Chapter Four

The first leg of the drive was dark, even for that time of the year. Clouds hung like wildfire smoke above us, ominous in the way they closed in more and more with the passing of each mile. It didn't help that Willa was driving. Her anxiety over whether or not we were going to be the last ones there was oozing right through her foot and into the accelerator. She weaved in and out of traffic like she was on Rainbow Road in Mario Kart.

"Easy," I said in a teasing voice. "You're gonna lose control with those small wrists."

She kept her eyes on the road. "Laugh all you want, but they're gonna come in handy at some point. Just watch."

"Sure."

"Good thing we're in a Toyota, right, Heath?" Mike said. "Safe and reliable as it gets."

One night I'd gotten blackout drunk and (supposedly) gone on this hour-long rant about why Mike should buy a Toyota, and he hadn't let me live it down since.

"Shut up, Mike," I said.

"I don't care how safe and reliable it is," Maggie said, Pinto sprawled on her lap and dead to the world. "I'm fucked if we get into a wreck. I don't have health insurance."

Maggie had recently been hired for a job at the Department of Agriculture. Two days later, the president shut the government down.

"Well, at the speeds we're going, I don't think you'll have to worry about uncovered medical expenses," Mike said. "At that point, we'll probably be dead."

"Shut up, Mike," Willa said.

"I'm tired of the abuse," he replied, his flat tone of voice unchanging. He pretended to go to sleep.

We hopped onto 421 North from I-40, and that's when the calls and texts started rolling in. Beau rang twice to ask us where we were—once from the toilet. Then Danielle. Then there was a Snapchat of Jake's bare ass. It wasn't even eight o'clock, but the mischief was well on its way in West Virginia. Some things never change.

"Good to know everybody's having a good time without us," Willa said. I could tell that she genuinely meant it, but the fear of missing out was strong with her. "How much longer to the gas station?" she asked.

I looked at the GPS on my phone. "Fifteen minutes."

My mind drifted into the centerlines of the road, and I thought about the last time I was in West Virginia. It smelled like no other place I'd ever been, and I think that was the coal. There was this bewitching grayness to the land. It was so cold that it hurt your bones, but there were swaths in the earth from which steam seemed to rise slowly and pale, like a cloud-cloaked sun on the winter horizon. The state may have considered itself

17

on the edge of Heaven, but my buddy said the Devil lived there. His grandpa said these were the last days.

That was ten years before, though. My friend and I had crossed into Wingo County and made a pit stop at a highway convenience store. The raddled lady behind the counter there was smoking a cigarette, and when we asked her if there were any restrooms, she took a puff and said, "They's a fence out back." We just looked at each other. I'll never forget that for as long as I live.

When we got to the gas station where Willa's parents were already waiting, I was fairly confident that there was a restroom inside, but I didn't look any further into it. We exited our cars, breath like plumes in the night.

"Hey, y'all," Willa's dad said, hugging my neck.

Her parents loved me, even though in their minds we were "living in sin." I had also long-harbored an unfounded suspicion that they didn't think I was good enough for her. She was going to school to be a scientist, and I was a Public Affairs Officer for the County—which was just a fancy way of saying that I wrote press releases any time a rabid raccoon was discovered on the side of the road.

"My Pinto Bean!" Willa's mom said, scooping up our dog and cradling him like a baby. "Hey, Maggie. Mike."

Both returned their hellos.

"How's your car runnin, honey?" Willa's dad asked. He had a nervous tic of adjusting his ball cap any time he talked.

"Good," she said. I could tell that she was impatient and ready to get back on the road.

"Good, good," he said. "Y'all be careful and don't get too drunk, now. You know what they say about those mountains—sometimes people go in, but they don't come back."

"Not funny," her mom replied.

He cracked a grin as I handed him Pinto's bag.

"I'll do my best to get your daughter back safe and sound," I said.

"What about us?" Mike asked.

"Can't make any promises there."

"Yeah, that might be too much to ask," Maggie added.

Willa fidgeted. "Well, we need to get going," she said. "We're gonna be the last ones there."

"All right, all right," her dad responded.

Willa turned the keys over to me for the second half of the drive. We said our goodbyes and jumped back into the car. I blew a kiss to Pinto and pulled off.

"I don't think we're gonna have many more opportunities to stop for food, guys," I said. "Y'all just wanna go ahead and get something while we're here?"

Everybody agreed, so I turned right out of the gas station parking lot and headed toward the Bojangles about a mile down the road. Once we got there, Mike took the opportunity to pack his one-hitter and smoked it in the parking lot. The sweet, skunky aroma capered on the air and delivered me to a different time and place, if only for a millisecond. Mike held out the pipe nonchalantly—like we weren't in public—inviting each of us to partake, but we all declined.

"God help you if my car smells like weed," Willa said.

The restaurant was fairly busy, though only three people seemed to be working behind the counter. We ordered our food and took our seats in the corner.

"You know, this would be a lot timelier if we could

just eat in the car," I said to Willa.

She buried me with her eyes. Laid me in the ground, shoveled dirt over the top. "My car is new," she said through gritted teeth. "I don't want it getting messy."

I smiled. Her fire was a contagion.

Mike and Maggie got their orders first. Then I got mine. Twenty minutes seemed to pass before Willa got hers, an unfortunate fact that only added to our ETA in Blue Brier. She was halfway through wolfing down her chicken tenders when a man walked in on the drive-thru-side door. He was tattered and rangy, a dancing expression of confusion on his chapped face. He moseyed from table to table, mumbling to himself, as if looking for something he'd lost. He made eye contact with me, but then quickly looked away again. Then he exited through the door on the other side. I glanced at Willa and Mike and Maggie. They hadn't noticed him.

When we returned to the SUV, the man was standing in the parking space next to ours. His matted hair riffled in the breeze. "Excuse me," he said.

A feeling of dread sank into my stomach.

"Y'all wouldn't happen to have a few dollars so I could get me somethin to eat, would you?" He held out his identification card from the VFW.

"Sorry, man," Mike said.

I was skeptical about whether or not he'd use the money for food. I considered asking him if I could buy him a meal instead, but we'd waited long enough for our food, and we were already late as it was. "I don't carry cash," I said.

He nodded, eyes as dark and glossy as volcanic glass. "Thank you anyway."

We got in the car, and Willa held out her bag of left-over french fries and a biscuit. "I was gonna eat this later, but I don't really need it," she said. "Give it to him."

"You sure?"

"Yeah."

I opened my door and approached the man. "I've got some fries and a biscuit, buddy," I said. "Do you want this?"

"Yessir, I do," he replied. He took the bag from my hand. Then he lingered there for longer than I expected he would, unnerving in the way that he was looking but not blinking. Like he was drilling for something. Whittling away flesh and judging what was underneath. "God bless y'all," he said. "Have a safe trip."

He turned and ambled toward the road. He really *had* been hungry. A feeling of shame came over me as I got back into the car. Why hadn't I just believed him? Why hadn't I taken him inside and bought him a combo? I could've left once I'd ordered and paid. It would have set us back five minutes at the most.

"That was nice," Maggie said as I strapped in.

I eased out of the parking lot and carried on toward the interstate. That's when it hit me. "Wait," I said. "He told me to have a safe trip. How'd he know we were going on a trip?"

"He probably saw our bags through the window," Willa said, downplaying my concern.

"Well, I feel bad for not doing more, but I got a weird vibe from that dude."

"That's a little problematic, don't you think?" Willa said.

I started to speak, but Maggie hollered, "Look out!"

A shadowy figure, longer than tall, darted across the road, and I had to swerve to avoid it. I whipped the SUV to the right and grabbed the steering wheel with both hands to steady it. When I peered out of the driver-side window, the black shape had disappeared into a row of houses on the other side of the road. It couldn't have been a dog; it was too big.

"What in the name of Christ was that?" I shouted.

"I couldn't get a good look at it," Mike replied.

Willa and Maggie agreed.

"Fucker came outta nowhere," I said, rubbing my chest.

I slowed to a stop at the intersection. There were signs for the interstate on my right. Next to them was the man from the Bojangles parking lot. Nobody said anything, but I could tell we were all looking at him. He stood there mannequinlike, holding the bag of food and wearing a smile on his face that was widening all the time. It wasn't a natural smile, and there was no earthly explanation for him being there. We had traveled at least two miles in a matter of minutes.

"Punch it," Willa said.

I floored the gas pedal when the light turned green and merged onto the highway, leaving the man in the rearview mirror. Or so I thought. When I looked into it, he wasn't there.

"I've got a serious question that I'm only gonna ask once, and then I'd like to leave it alone forever," Maggie said. "Am I the only one who couldn't see the pupils in his eyes just now?"

Chapter Five

I moved back in with my mom two weeks after the phone call, took a job at a grocery store, and told myself I'd be back in class within a year. But then I continued to live like I had in school. I spent the next five years going out to local bars almost every night, blacking out and making an ass of myself wherever I darkened a door. I slept in until two or three o'clock in the afternoon, or whenever it was that my shift started, sometimes unsure of how I'd gotten in my bed. I got into fights with my mother on a daily basis. On one such occasion, she barged into my room and started collecting dirty clothes from the floor.

"You gonna get up today, son?" she asked. "It's goin on 3:30."

I rolled toward the window, turning my back to her. Spears of sunlight spilled through the window blinds and onto my shut eyes. "It's my day off," I said into my pillow.

"You'd think you'd wanna do somethin with it, then," she said.

"I am," I replied curtly. I didn't know that I hated myself yet, but I did. It was a feeling that was knotting inside me insidiously, for how long I can't say.

"What happened to reapplying to school?"

There was something supercilious in her tone that didn't particularly sit well with me. "I'm working on it," I said, sitting up. "What are you doing in here anyway? You can't just come into my room unannounced; I'm a grown-ass man."

She shot me the same look she'd given me when I was a small child. Like when we were at the store and I was touching things I wasn't supposed to be touching. She said, "This is still my house. I pay the bills."

If I had anything to say, I bit it back and stared straight ahead, woolly-eyed.

"I'm worried about you, son," my mother continued. "It's been three years, and you haven't gone back like you promised. You seem content to wallow around here all day. And you blow every last cent of your paycheck at the bar."

"That's not true."

"Well, when's the last time you offered to give me rent?" She waited, but she knew the answer wasn't going to come.

"I'll do better," I said, and my words sounded as empty as they felt. A crumpled aluminum tallboy can cast aside in the gutter.

"I hope so," she said, balancing the laundry basket. She left the room and closed the door behind her.

I threw my pillow at the wall; it smacked limply and puckered to the floor. The self-loathing welled up inside me like poison around a bite. I knew my mother was right. This wouldn't be the last quarrel. Not by a mile. In the time after, she would invite me to church, but I'd decline her invitation every time. I was miserable, and I blamed her for it. I resented her for something I'd done to myself. And one day, I let her know it.

Chapter Six

We crossed into Virginia forty-five minutes after the Yadkinville Bojangles incident, all of us still rattled by what we'd seen. None of us had much to say, and so there was only the hum of the engine and spinning tires on the uneven interstate asphalt. I'd been through Virginia several times on the way to D.C. or Maryland or Pennsylvania and found it to be a serene but dull state, with never-ending bends of shortleaf pines and carbon copy roads.

That's actually a euphemism. I detested Virginia. To me, it was just hours upon hours of useless state, same-looking people and same-looking places. That's the only way I knew how to describe it. There *had* to be more to it than that.

"I hate this place," I said.

For a moment, I thought no one was going to humor me. But Mike didn't let me down. "How can you hate a state that's slogan literally says it's for lovers?" he asked.

I sighed and took a sip of my Coke Zero. I was

already getting antsy. The comedown was coming on.

"Well, I think I have my answer," Mike said.

I reached for the volume knob on the radio, hoping to make our time in Old Dominion more bearable, but when I turned it clockwise, I was met with the crackling of static.

"Seems on par for the course," I said.

I must have flipped through a dozen or more stations, each with the same result: a fuzzy, unvarying compilation of sound waves that seemed to serve as a spot-on representation for our current journey. Stretches of road begetting stretches of road, vapid and dark and purgatorial. I was seconds from calling it quits when I picked up something. Ever-so-clearly, John Denver's "Take Me Home, Country Roads" began to seep through the speakers. I didn't consider the irony at first.

"Now we're talking," Maggie said.

I wasn't a fan myself, but even I had to admit that it was at least something. Everybody sang along except for me. They sang about the Shenandoah. They sang about the very mountains we were punching through at that moment. About the middle ground between old and young life, the vibrance of ancient things made new again.

I rolled my eyes, and Willa winked at me.

The mood had taken a turn for the better in the car. But when the second verse started, the singing tapered off. A voice that at least sounded like it belonged to John Denver continued: "I was lost once, but by faith was found. Shouted glory, Hallelujah, like a hound. My redeemer come down and rescued me. If you don't repent now, you will never leave."

For a moment, we all looked at the touchscreen display, then at each other.

"I've never heard this version before," Mike said.

John Denver kept going, his voice growing warbly and distant. Halfway through the chorus, it was almost otherworldly in its distortion. He pleaded with his native land to carry him back to where it all began, those famous words so unrecognizable. I changed the station and found myself relieved by the calm of the static. Then, four or five channels later, we heard it again. There were now spaces between the words, and there was no accompanying music. Only nefariously nostalgic lyrics yearning for a homecoming.

"What kind of backwoods ass cover is this?" Maggie asked.

There was a pang in my stomach as I pushed the power button to kill the music. "What is it with tonight?" I asked.

Nobody had anything to say this time. Not even Mike.

We sat in silence for several minutes, carving through the Blue Ridge Mountains towering on either side of us, unseen and nebulous in the deadness of the day. These natural landforms had always greeted me as gentle giants, but now they bore a sense of secretiveness and hostility. I felt trapped in between them—claustrophobic, though that wasn't a specific fear of mine. Not yet. As we drove, I noticed that the mountainsides were sprinkled with little lights, and I figured those were houses. Perhaps they were signaling back and forth. Maybe they were using those twinkling gold lanterns to let each other know that they weren't alone out there in the dark.

But I also saw lights that weren't gold. Two of them. They were distinctly red, a deep vermilion, and they were grouped together like a fresh snakebite that had

28

just begun to discharge blood. And in the same breath, they faded into the void; I thought maybe they'd never been there to begin with. Of course, my eyes could have been playing tricks on me; I'd been up since five-thirty that morning.

"I'm gonna need to get fucked up after this drive," Maggie chimed in, right on time.

All of us shared that sentiment. For the next hour, we made small talk as we made our way northward along I-81, and one mountain chain became another. Willa relayed updates on the situation at the house via Danielle and Livy and tried to fight off sleep. Maggie talked about her father's barbecue side hustle. Mike threw in a few dad jokes. Anything to keep our minds off of how disturbing the drive had been to that point.

We passed an enormous industrial plant on our left, the smoke of which submerged the approaching Alleghenies like an underwater mountain range. "Coal?" I asked to no one in particular.

"Chemical manufacturing," Mike said.

"Oh, that's right. You work at one of these places, don't you?"

"When the well gets low," he responded.

"Welcome to West Virginia," the smooth voice of the GPS announced.

There was a collective sigh of relief in the car.

"Thank God," Maggie said.

I didn't go that far.

Narrow mountain curves marked our first ten minutes in the state. The Monongahela National Forest stretched out on either side of us for an indeterminable distance. I hadn't noticed before, but it suddenly occurred to me that the shoulders of the road were lined with small piles of snow. Every so often, I felt the tires

29

catch on a random smattering.

Mike mumbled something from the backseat after about the third or fourth time this happened.

"You all right?" Willa asked.

"Yeah, I just get anxious around sharp turns," he said. "I'll be good."

"Well, it's supposed to snow again Sunday morning," I said. "Imagine this, but like, the roads covered in ice." I even motioned with my hands to really drive the point home.

Willa cut her eyes at me. "Why would you say something like that to him, Heath? He already told you he's nervous." Willa was always standing up for people. It's something I admired about her.

"Sorry, Mike," I replied, a tinge embarrassed. I really didn't know why I had said that.

"No harm, no foul," he said. "I'm just still fairly baked."

We finally came upon what looked like a town, but I couldn't read its sign at the time. I assumed it was Blue Brier since we were only fifteen minutes or so out. We passed a gas station with an off-brand pizza restaurant inside of it. A Russian doll of American business outfits. Both were closed.

"What kind of hick shit is that?" I asked.

"Oh, so we're demonizing the homeless *and* rural communities now?" Willa said. "How lovely."

"Are you kidding me?" Maggie said. "I love a good slice of gas station pizza, but that homeless man demonized himself."

We drove by a car shop, a mini-mart, a drugstore, and a statue dedicated to the Blue Brier Sons of the Confederacy. It was front and center on the lawn of what could only be the local magistrate's office.

"Great," Willa said.

"Not so self-righteous now, are you?" I teased.

A light fog began to set in as we neared houses. Some of them were quite nice—small but designed with dashes of Greek Revival architecture. Others were old and rundown and vernacular, and they made me question whether or not anyone lived in them at all. Sparse street lights shone on the signs in their snow-spattered yards. One of them read:

JESUS IS COMING.

Another:

ARE YOU READY?

A strong sense of déjà vu washed over me and nestled into my conscience, taking shape as pieces and memories from my hometown.

"Turn from thy wicked ways," I read. "Hmm. Hospitable."

There was at least some part of me that got it, though. These were tough times. The world had gone to shit—to Hell in a handbasket—and a lot of people were scared that it was only going to get worse until life as we knew it reached a breaking point. Many were convinced that the end was nigh, and the idea of Christ comforted them. They were covered by The Blood. Some part of me—albeit the smallest fragment—found that endearing.

"Where to from here?" I asked.

Maggie, who had taken over GPS duties, studied her phone. "You're gonna turn right onto the Aylett Mercer Parkway in a half-mile," she said. "Then sharp left onto Yellow Sulfur Springs Road right after that. Then another quick left onto Mouth of Sheol Road. That's where the house should be."

"What the hell kind of names are those?" I asked. "What's our destination, the Twilight Zone?"

"Apparently, it's Mouth of Sheol," Mike said.

"Thank you, Mike."

Structures became few and far between as we ascended the General Aylett Mercer Memorial Parkway and hung an immediate left onto Yellow Sulfur Springs. We approached a four-way intersection soon after, a dilapidated, haunted-looking building on our right, an abyssal chasm directly ahead. That's when we lost GPS signal. *Phenomenal*, I thought to myself as I eased onto the brakes and flipped on the brights. I squinted at the street sign to my left. It was well-weathered but still readable:

UNINCORPORATED MOUTH OF SHEOL

That was good enough for me. I swiveled the steering wheel left, entering a tight one-way gravel road. We inched along, tires crunching on the stones underneath. And then there was a noticeable bump.

"What was that?" Willa asked.

"It's almost like we're on a mountain," Mike said.

"Mike."

"No, she's right," I said. "That didn't feel right."

I put the car in park.

"What are you doing?" Willa asked.

"I'm gonna check it out."

"Please don't go out there, Heath," she said.

"I'm just gonna make sure everything is all right with your tires."

I opened the door and stepped out of the car. I could feel the gooseflesh develop as I switched on my phone's flashlight. I tip-toed three paces to the left before I saw it. A coyote lay sprawled and whimpering on its side by the bumper of the SUV, its blood-matted fur still tacky. There were tread marks on its flattened back half, I guess from where I had run over it, and the sight of this made me wince. But that's not what put it there in the first place. Something had gotten to its neck with grisly, mortal gashes. It shifted its eyes at me without turning its head. It was breathing a mile a minute.

I poked my head inside the cabin. "It's a coyote," I said.

"Is it still alive?" Willa asked.

"Barely."

"Oh, Jesus, did we hit it?" she asked, tears welling in her eyes.

"Yeah, but trust me, something got it before we did."

"That's comforting," Mike said.

I didn't bat an eye at that. We were out in the boonies, and I imagined that shit killed other shit out here all the time.

Willa cupped her mouth. "We can't just leave it here, Heath."

I turned my attention toward the animal again. Then I removed the pocketknife from my jacket and crouched down next to it. It really was a sad sight, and I was conflicted about whether or not I should put it out of its misery. I'd taken life before—deer mostly—but I'd cried every time. My relationship with coyotes was also more complicated. I grew up in a suburban area, but every once in a while, they found their way into the neighborhood. I'd long-suspected one of killing my childhood dog, and I'd never gotten over that. But I didn't want to let a living thing suffer, either. It whined at me now, and it reminded me of the time Pinto had gotten a thorn lodged in his paw pads. It was one of the most pitiful sounds I had ever heard. If I hadn't known any better, I'd say it was begging me to get it over with.

I thought about the blade of my knife. Imagined the shredding noise it would make as it tore through the pelt and the flesh and severed the jugular vein. The visceral feeling that would start in my hand and reverberate through my bones, the eyes of the coyote falling lifeless and still in the finality of that moment. I pictured the spurting blood as it stained the gravel path. A bubble crept into my throat as I looked over the animal, end-to-end. And I decided I couldn't go through with it. It would die soon enough as it was.

I rose to my feet and returned the knife to its pocket. I reached into the other pocket, withdrew a pill bottle, and turned it into my mouth. I savored the grittiness as the tablet dissolved on my tongue. A funny thing, going through life sedated. I expelled a deep breath and got back in the car. Nobody said anything, but they didn't have to. They wanted to know what had happened.

"It's done," I said, a cold, shameful lie.

Willa sniffled. "Poor baby."

We continued up Mouth of Sheol Road, wondering if the night would ever end.

Chapter Seven

I never understood the point of open-casket funerals and visitations. In my mind, they only added grief to a process already chock-full of it. My mother looked bloated. Her eyelids were glued horizontally, and the hard striations of her skin were plastered over. Her lips were shriveled inward like a person from a photograph that was taken before it was normal to smile.

She lay in the middle of a room with hideous wallpaper and an odor that was too sterile for comfort. It smelled the way my kindergarten classroom had smelled on the first day of school. But that's what she wanted. She couldn't stand the idea of being burned up, even though she wouldn't be alive to witness it. I was alive, though. Nothing made me more conscious of that fact than looking upon her pale, stiff body and the folded hands that had held me with so much love and warmth as a baby.

I stood there next to her—face hardened by dried tears—as distraught as I was hungover. A line formed at the foot of her casket and stretched across the room to the entrance of the parlor. She didn't have many remaining family members, and so the overwhelming majority of her visitors were from work or church. They shook my hand and spoke in empty words or Bible verses. Maybe both. Some went as far as to hug me or offer their ears any time I needed them.

Some guy my mom went to high school with showed up wearing a denim jacket and smelling like a fully smoked carton of Marlboro Reds. "Damn shame," he said, adjusting the toothpick in his mouth.

I nodded.

"Was she saved?" he asked.

I didn't answer right away, but when I did, it felt especially cold. "She went to church," I said.

The man, unsavory as he was, offered a polite smile before he took the hint and moved on.

I looked at my mom. Saved. That word meant nothing to me.

Once the last person had paid their respects and the last ladleful of Cheerwine punch had been consumed, I turned toward my mother. I gripped the handle of the casket with both hands, and I could feel my shirt glued to my back and shoulders by a fresh varnishing of sweat. I wanted to tell her I was sorry. I wanted to tell her a lot of things, but every time the words crept up to my lips, they tripped and tumbled backward over my tongue and rolled down my throat into the pit of my stomach, where they would forever lie like a fossil escaping excavation for eon after eon.

The funeral home director closed the double doors of the room. "Take as much time as you want," he told me, patting me on my arm.

I hung my head over the casket. And then something happened that I've never told anyone about.

Chapter Eight

We had gone two miles on the cramped gravel road before we saw the first house. It was a yellow double-wide that looked like it had been beat to shit by decades of winter fury. A fairly new, black, heavy-duty pickup truck sat parked to the side, and just beyond that, there was a ramshackle shed with a white canvas tarp draped over it. In the light created by my high beams, I could read what was written on it in thick, spray-painted letters:

PREPARE TO MEET THY GOD

"Wow, they really like their Bible out here, don't they?" Willa said.

"They certainly seemed to have narrowed down their favorite parts," I added.

"This is some *Hills Have Eyes* shit," Maggie whispered, loud enough to be heard. "I mean, I go to church, but damn."

Perhaps this shouldn't have come as a shock to us.

Being from North Carolina, we weren't strangers to a doomy piece of prophecy or two. On church bulletins, on billboards. Even at public schools in some cases. Still, we were in the Bible Belt, and Blue Brier seemed to be the buckle.

Another mile or so came and went. The path was slick with snow dust, and the fog was thickening by the second. Starved tree limbs, sinuous and naked, sliced through the haze to either side of us. They were our only company out here in this world of never-ending shadows—until we stumbled upon a fork in the road.

"Dammit," I said, putting the car in park. "Do you remember if we're supposed to bear left or keep right, Maggie?"

"I really don't know."

"Danielle said we'd come upon a gate that looks like a park entrance," Willa said. "It should be open."

But I barely heard her. I was too busy focusing on what I saw to my left. A lone, muted porch light cut through the fog and illuminated a dinky shack with a wooden-planked roof. A slender, silhouetted figure, arms at its sides, stood in front of the building, as still as an artist's model. Sylphlike. Watching something. Watching us. It was a woman.

"Sweet Christ," Maggie said.

I listened to the rumble of the idling engine and played an internal game of tug of war over what I was about to do next. I placed my knife on my lap and rolled down my window. "Excuse me," I shouted.

I could feel everyone's eyes fall upon me.

"Are you fucking crazy?" Maggie said.

"I'm just gonna ask her for directions," I replied.

"Have you never seen a horror movie, Heath?" she asked, panic leaking into her voice.

"Yeah, this doesn't feel right," Willa said.

"Excuse me," I repeated, louder.

The lady started moving our way with a short, measured gait. Her feet waded forward, but she didn't make a sound. Her posture didn't change. There was something mechanical about it.

"I just wanna know which part of this sounds like a good idea," Maggie said.

"Let me handle this," I said. "It'll be okay."

As the lady drew within ten feet, I could make out most of her features. She looked to be in her early sixties and dressed in dirty planter's coveralls. Her curly hair was wet, as if she'd been standing in the rain all day, and her face was almost vacuous. Like she'd never felt joy but hadn't felt pain, either. She stopped an arm's length away.

"How are you?" I asked with a cautious smile.

She responded with a simple nod.

"We're looking for a house at the end of this road. Do you know if we keep going right here or if we turn left?"

"I vote we go wherever the fuck she's not," Maggie whispered in the back.

"You're supposed to be on Mouth of Sheol?" the lady asked, her voice a little more than a mumble.

"Yes, ma'am," I said.

"Do y'all know what Sheol means?" she asked. I couldn't be certain, but it looked as though she had bloomed a little grin.

"No, ma'am." I repressed the answer I wanted to give. I wanted to tell her no, and that I didn't give a shit.

"There's a house at the end of this road, all right," she said. Then she stared off as if she'd lost her train of thought.

Willa squeezed my right hand.

"Ma'am?"

"Have you seen the dog?" she asked, still looking off, her drawl more of a gasp than anything. Her skin held the color of something bloodless.

"The dog?"

"The dog," she repeated. "There was a time when Yahweh went yonder to the netherworld to bring sinners back with him," she continued. "But soon as he come to the gate, the dog was there waitin for him."

"Oh, hell no," Maggie said.

"Now, Yahweh don't try no more on account of he knows it's no use. Them people have to fend for themselves in all that sulfur and brimstone." She was still turned away. "The dog. I seen him somewhere."

Willa moved the gear shift into drive.

The darkness was with us now. It had been there in the background for the duration of the ride, but now it was a part of us. It settled into our hearts, festering and unforgiving, and there was a sound to it, and that sound was as sorrowful as anything any of us had ever heard. Even the headlamps of the SUV seemed dim in this doleful scene playing out before us like a requiem for light.

The lady turned toward me, her mouth quivered. Her already-pale complexion gave up its last ghost. Then she began to speak gibberish—not quite in tongues, but it was close enough.

"Dude, let's get the fuck outta here," Mike said. "I'm too high for this shit."

I'd heard enough myself. I tore off toward the right, leaving the lady in the dust. For all I knew, I was throwing rocks at her, but that was just as well in my mind. The path became less visible in the growing fog; I couldn't see further than three feet in front of me—if that. Nor could I see behind me, which wasn't necessarily a bad thing.

"I could kill you, Heath," Maggie said. The skin beneath her freckles was bright red.

"I'm sorry."

"So we can all agree that she was a fucking lunatic and that we shouldn't have asked her for directions, right?"

"Well, I didn't see anybody else making any kind of decision," I snapped. "Maybe the fucking coyote we ran over was the dog she was talking about."

But I didn't believe it.

There was a palpable sense of tension in the car now. I tried not to think about Yadkinville, but I did all the same. About the thing that bolted across the road. I doubt I was the only one who did, but still, I pushed it into the back of my mind, shut the door on it, and duct-taped the creases. Only a paranoid madman would think that it was all connected. But only a delusional fool wouldn't have noticed the coincidence.

It was another two blurry miles before we arrived at the gate, which was exactly as Danielle had described it: black poles, red and white reflectors. Something you'd see at a public park. It was open, so I drove through. A quarter-mile uphill we came into a clearing of trampled grass. Three vehicles were parked there, and directly behind them was the house from the online pictures. We had lucked out and guessed right.

A sigh escaped someone, but I couldn't tell whom. Maybe all of us.

I popped the hatch, and we got out, squelching onto the muddied grass beneath our feet. As I sorted through our belongings, I whiffed the air. It smelled so strongly of sulfur that you'd think a fireworks display had just occurred right there on that mountain.

Chapter Nine

After my mother's funeral, I didn't get out of bed for two weeks. The grocery store had given me three days of bereavement pay, but I never went back. I contemplated killing myself more times than I care to share, but I could never go through with it. I was too much of a coward. It sounds foolish now, but as a kid I'd been told that suicide resulted in immediate damnation with no hope for redemption. I've never been able to cut ties with that paranoia.

So in the absence of an out, I handled things the only way I knew how: pills. I had developed a taste for uppers in school to help me concentrate on my homework. They worked magic when the weed made me too spacey. I'd also happened into a love affair with prescription anxiety meds to bring me back down to Earth. They afforded me a pleasant, desensitized low when I felt like removing myself from the rest of the world. They were my invisibility.

Without my mother or my job, speed was the only thing that dragged me out of bed in the morning, and benzodiazepines were the only reason I'd get back in it at the end of the day. I drank heavily on the week-ends, milking my mother's life insurance policy—or what was left of it after I buried her—to keep the lights on. I didn't know where to go from there, and I figured I'd waste away eventually, no matter what I did. But then I found purpose in a promise I'd made. It came to me in the middle of a hot, restless night like a cool drink of water:

"I want you to promise me, right here and now, that if you do this, you'll go back and finish."

I had said that I would, and so I did. I sold my mother's house and set up shop in a studio apartment in Greensboro. I enrolled in the local college as a Pub-lic Policy major, whatever the hell that means, and jumped back in headfirst. I did well, too. I was named to the Dean's List after my first few semesters, and de-spite my destructive habits, I excelled in my summer classes as well. A functional junkie. But the loneliness that followed me was all-consuming; it eclipsed my every step like a shadow that I couldn't shake loose no matter how fast I ran.

Then I met Willa in English class in the fall semes-ter of 2017. Our first exchange went something like this:

"I appreciate how you weren't afraid to call out Hemingway as a misogynist," she said as we exited the classroom and made for the courtyard of North campus. "Everybody else seemed content to bow at the altar of his bullshit."

"I take it you're not a fan," I said.

"His writing is beautiful, but I can't get behind his characterization of women," she replied. "He pulls the victim card too much, and he's a narcissist."

"Have you read *Hills Like White Elephants*?" I asked

as we came into a clearing in the courtyard.

The sunlight sent shafts of blooming light through her brown eyes, and I couldn't get over how kind they were. "No, but if you have a copy, I'd be glad to read it and get back to you."

"Cool," I said. "What's your email address?"

She glanced at me a little sideways. "How about my phone number?"

I started to say that I couldn't send an entire story via text message, but then I got the hint. She would continue to rag me about the email thing for months to come.

We were dating within a couple of weeks, and once undergrad was over, we relocated to Durham for her grad school. We got a dog together. She introduced me to her friends. Willa was beautiful and genuine and fiery. She was everything I didn't know I needed. For a while, I thought I was living my second life, but it was the first one all the same. The guilt and depression had never left me. And I was using the same coping mechanisms as I had all along.

Chapter Ten

I remember standing there out front, watching my breath in the cold night like a child pretending to exhale cigarette smoke. I thought it was too quiet in the house. And I was right. We entered the front door and found ourselves not in a common area, but rather one of the six bedrooms. There were bags and coats on the king-sized bed, but no other suggestions that anyone was there. There was no chatter or laughter in the walls—only the quiet, unoccupied space of a ghost town. More importantly, there was no music. I'd never been to a get-together with Willa's friends that wasn't scored by some random, blaring playlist.

We checked the other two upstairs bedrooms, both similar to the first, and the living room, an open area with a leather loveseat, a futon, and an ugly pullout couch that separated it from the kitchen. No cigar. The house itself was rather cozy and inviting upon first glance. It looked like a year-round family home rather than a seasonal retreat for rowdy postgrads and twenty-somethings. A mahogany entertainment center stood catty-cornered to the living room's long picture window. In the opposite corner sat an antique Singer sewing machine, one of those turn-of-the-century models with the steel flywheel and treadle attached to the table. The kitchen light was on, and there were sheets of half-eaten food on the stove, but no sign that there had been anyone there to cook it.

Willa opened a cracked door just off the living room, revealing a set of downward-leading stairs. We dropped our bags and descended them into a dimly lit den with a roomy recreation area fit for a bachelor. There was a flat-screen TV and a gas fireplace in front of a comfy-looking sectional sofa. Behind it, there was a ping-pong table adorned with red Solo cups and a putting green. But still, no people.

Yep, I thought to myself. *We'd done it. We'd survived the creepiest car ride in the history of car rides only to arrive at Roanoke Island and find CROATOAN carved into a fence post.*

Maggie lifted her hands and dropped them in exasperation. Then there was a noise, so low that we could have imagined it. I pushed through the French doors at the right of the putting green and stepped into a tiny corridor that produced four more doors, two on each side. The noise came again. It was the sound of voices. I turned the knob on the door at the back right, Willa and Mike and Maggie in a line behind me, and was greeted by a slurry of hollers. Like the big reveal at a surprise birthday party.

They were all there, cast in the incandescent purple of a blacklight. Almost everybody, at least. Some were on the two twin beds. Freddie and Livy. Andy and Eden. Others were on the floor. Danielle. Beau. And, yes, Delco.

"Y'all come on in," Beau said, beckoning aggressively with one hand. There were two beer cans in the other. He patted me on the back. "We thought y'all was lost as last year's Easter eggs."

"Don't even get me started," Maggie said.

Danielle closed the door behind us.

"What's all this?" Willa asked.

"We come down here to have a heart-to-heart," Beau said. His eyes were as amiable and boozy as ever. "We've been takin turns gettin in our feels. Positive vibes only."

"Positive vibes only," Delco repeated, his accent more pronounced and drawn out than usual. Alcohol will do that.

"Who's next?" Beau asked.

I leaned against a dresser, gripping my brown-bagged bottle of Pinot Noir and feeling a bit pretentious. Feeling *a lot* pretentious, actually. Willa, Mike, and Maggie took seats on the floor.

"I'll go, I'll go," Andy said in his smooth-talking tone as if he was being forced. He had the confident mien of someone twice his age, and he spoke with the cadence of a salesman, which was appropriate considering that he was in law school at the time.

Beau shushed everyone.

"I just wanna say that I'm thankful for everybody in this room," Andy went on. "Four-ish years, two drinking tickets, and a couple of withheld security deposits later," he paused for laughter, his too-perfect teeth shining like glow sticks, "and we're all still together." He held his beer up in a toast. "You guys are the best."

Everyone received his words well. They responded with claps and cheers.

"Boom!" Delco cried, an unintelligible endorsement.

I probably looked at him like I'd just tasted something sour. I've never had a convincing poker face.

Andy kissed Eden, his fiancé, a pretty, full-figured blonde who happened to be closer to my age than his. She was soft-spoken, though she had been a college valedictorian somewhere in South Carolina.

"Mike next," Delco blurted, and everyone agreed.

Mike rose to his feet, hands at the ready like he expected to faceplant onto the floor.

"Nobody told you to stand, Mike," Willa teased through cupped hands.

"I know, but I like to live dangerously," he replied, as dry as a piece of unbuttered toast.

Delco cackled. His laugh was somewhere between a stoner's giggle and the reaction of someone who's late to the joke but doesn't want to be left out.

"I'll keep it short and sweet," Mike said, his eyes stoned, lucent. "We've known each other for over four years. We've been through a lot together. And none of you have killed me in my sleep yet. Cheers." He sat down.

Everyone raised their drinks.

"That was beautiful," Andy said.

For the briefest of moments, I found myself lost in the neon swirls of the blacklight poster on the adjacent wall of the room. It was a nature scene with a vibrant green dale, howling red wolves, and electric blue butterflies beneath a moon that looked full-blown and possessed. I remember thinking about how uncharacteristic this room was compared to the rest of the house. It was reflective of how I felt about my place in this strange conference.

Maggie went next. Then Willa. Both were probably

heartfelt and articulate, but if they were, I didn't hear them. My mind meandered back to my Organizational Speech class in college and how I'd nearly passed out before every presentation. As scary and nerve-racking as our drive to West Virginia had been, it now paled in comparison to the thought of having to form words with several eyes on me. Or the idea of having to open up, something I'd struggled with since childhood.

The benzo I'd taken was starting to kick in, smoothing over my nerves like a hot clothes iron on a wrinkled shirt. But I was still uncomfortable talking in front of groups—even if they were composed of people I knew—and nothing was going to change that. I'd read somewhere once that most people would rather die than speak in public, and I found that believable.

My thoughts were interrupted by Beau's voice. "You're up, Heath," he said. "Lay it on us, buddy."

I scratched my nose, my heart hammering in my chest as if my rib bones were railroad spikes. "Well, anyone who knows me knows I'm not in the habit of getting sappy," I started. I could feel the wobble in my words. "But ever since I met Willa, you guys have accepted me as one of your own." I paused to think. I studied their glowing faces. It was coming easier now, and it was surprisingly genuine. "You've been quick to welcome and slow to judge. I'm grateful for that."

The last sentence didn't feel entirely wrong. There was a gap between Willa's friends and me—there always would be—but in that moment, it didn't feel as broad as it had in the past. It was corny, sure, but I felt like I'd shared a grain of truth with them that I wouldn't get back. I felt vulnerable, but I didn't cringe like I was apt to do in those sorts of situations. There was something intimate about it. Maybe I was just caught in the euphoria of having survived that nightmarish road trip.

Nobody said anything, but I could tell they were smiling.

"Heath, you're a star," Danielle said in her zany lilt. She reminded me of an old-timey comic who specialized in one-liners.

"Amen," Beau agreed.

One of the three inevitable awkward silences that every party suffers at some point through the night came on quick and unannounced.

Beau raised his fist. "Now, let's go get fucked up."

His command was met with an enthusiastic whoop as everyone hopped to their feet and filtered into the corridor. I trickled in behind them, and just as I got to the French doors of the den, the side door on the left swung open, nearly hitting me. I heard the sound of a refilling toilet as Jake staggered out and brushed into me.

"Hey, watch yours—" he slurred. "Oh, hey man, what's up?" He hugged me. "When did y'all get here?"

"Just a minute ago," I said. He smelled like a distillery. "Damn, dude. There any liquor left upstairs?"

"Bro, I just threw up," he confirmed in his plain, unabashed manner of speech. He put his arm around my neck. "You wanna take a shot?"

I motioned toward my bottle and laughed. "I'm gonna start with this, and we'll go from there."

"Bet." He glanced over my shoulder. When he saw that the bedroom was empty, he stumbled through the den and toward the stairs.

We climbed them and joined everyone in the living room.

Delco grimaced by the kitchen island and removed a lime from his mouth. "Hey, Jake. You done yacking, you fortune cookie-eating motherfucker?"

Jake stopped in his tracks and swayed where he stood. "I'm Cambodian, you dumbass." He always rolled with the punches, no matter how offensive or tasteless they were. And sometimes, he threw his own.

I shook my head and grabbed my bookbag.

"Heath," Willa called from the doorway directly behind the pullout couch. "We're over here."

Our bedroom for the weekend was homey, albeit much too humid for comfort. I unshouldered my bag onto the queen-sized bed and pored over some of the wall art. It was pretty standard watercolor stuff. A steeple in the heart of a valley. A prairie homestead in the dead of winter. Deer grazing in fields of white clover. There was also an 8x5 reproduction of a painting of Jesus praying in the Garden of Gethsemane on the nightstand. I turned it facedown.

"Hey," Willa said. She gently wrapped her hands around my waist as I turned to her. "I'm sorry for being on edge earlier."

I moved a strand of hair from her face. "I'm sorry, too."

"We're gonna have a good weekend?"

"You bet," I said, kissing her. "I'm gonna have to pop a window in here, though, because it's hotter than Hell."

Chapter Eleven

We huddled in with everyone around the kitchen bar, where Andy, Jake, Danielle, Delco, Maggie, and Livy had just finished taking shots. Beer cans, cigarette packs, flakes of weed, baggies, and several unidentified powder substances littered the counter. There were also bottles of liquor and wine—ten that I could count. I added mine to the collection.

"Pretty sweet, ain't it?" Beau said in front of a hiccup. He was eyeballing a small laundry room off the back corner of the kitchen that I hadn't noticed before.

"Yeah, this place is really nice," Willa said.

Beau panned the room. "I wasn't too sure on account of it didn't have any reviews on HomeAway and all, but I reckon we done pretty good."

No reviews? Something about that didn't sit well with me, but I kept it to myself. I had a bad habit of interjecting with unpopular opinions enough as it was.

"We weren't sure what we were gonna walk into, either," Maggie said. "Not after the way that car ride went."

"What was that all about, anyway?" Beau asked.

"Let's see, where should I start?" Maggie said. "We ran into a homeless man with no pupils in his eyeballs. Then we almost hit a dog." She held up her fingers and counted them off. "We heard a cover of 'Take Me Home, Country Roads' that sounded like David Koresh recorded it. Heath killed a coyote. Then the cherry on top of the cake was running into this batshit lady just up the road."

"Wait," Delco interrupted. He drew from his vape pen. "You killed a coyote?"

I felt put on the spot, and I guess I was. "I had to," I said. "It was just gonna die slow otherwise." Suddenly, I was eaten up with the guilt of the lie all over again.

"That's pretty fuckin gnarly, dude," Delco replied.

"Killing a dying creature?" Willa questioned.

"Well, yeah," Delco said, an off-putting little smirk etched into his face. "I mean, I've never killed any-thing."

"I wouldn't recommend it," I responded coldly. In my mind, the coyote's moribund gaze located me again, eyes wet and jittery and pleading for mercy.

There was an awkward silence, but then Beau res-cued us from it. "I'm sorry you had to do that, Heath. But I'm sure it was the right thing." He sipped one of his beers. "What's this about a batshit lady, though?"

"When we got to the fork in the road a few miles back, there was this shady old woman standing in her yard," Willa explained. "Heath asked her for directions."

"It was a bold strategy," Mike added.

"What'd she say?" Beau asked.

"She went on this bit about a dog that keeps God from stealing sinners out of the underworld, or some nonsense," I said. "I don't know; I couldn't really keep up."

"You mean a hellhound?"

I raised my head to find Freddie snacking on a mozzarella stick by the oven. "What was that?" I asked him.

"A hellhound," he said, wiping his fingers on a paper towel. "It's from the Harrowing of Hell. In some sects of Christian theology, there's this belief that Jesus literally descended into Hell during the three days between the Crucifixion and the Resurrection. And when he rose, he brought back souls with him that woulda otherwise been lost forever. But legend says that he had to get past a beast that guarded the gate. A hellhound. Lots of cultures have adopted their own versions of it."

"Where'd you learn that?" I asked.

Freddie lifted his hands like he didn't know what to do with them and smiled. "Google?"

Beau butted in. "Well, I don't know nothin about helldogs, but the owner of this place *did* mention somethin about black bears in her email."

"Either way, it was the spookiest five hours of my life," Maggie huffed. "And I'll take black bears over that any day of the week."

"Well, you're here now," Beau said, winking harmlessly and tapping his beer against Maggie's. "So, put it behind you."

"I'll drink to that," she said.

Jake, who had looked so immersed in meditation that he may as well have been pondering his life's purpose, turned to me. He considered me like he hadn't just seen me in the hallway; he looked me up and down. "Man, that boy thicc," he said. Then he belched and dropped his chin again.

I shook my head and stepped into the kitchen,

hunting for a pair of scissors. I found some in a drawer next to the sink and used them to clip the mouthpiece of my cigar. Then I fished a corkscrew from the same drawer of random utensils and got to work on my bottle of wine.

"Vino Heath!" Andy hollered.

I felt myself flush a little behind a smile as I buried the corkscrew into the bottle and pulled up. Vino Heath was a nickname they'd bestowed upon me because I was apparently more fun to be around when I drank wine. I didn't see or feel the difference, but I went along with it all the same.

"Vino Heath," Danielle repeated. In Willa's words, Danielle yelled but not yelled when she'd been drinking, and she was in true form on this night. She was bubbly and black-haired, and her expressions were always affectionate yet discerning. It was easy to see why she and Jake would probably always be together.

I lifted my Solo cup in concession and bee-lined it toward the sliding glass door behind the ten-top dinner table, hoping to find a quiet place to decompress. I stepped onto the wraparound porch, the last murmur of voices escaping as I slipped the door back in place behind me. The fog was dense and lazy, and the stench of sulfur still lay thick on the air as I rolled my cigar against the flame of the lighter in my fingers. Once I got it going in a steady, albeit weak, burn, I approached the railing ahead of me and gazed upon the starless horizon. There wasn't the slightest hint of a cloud or mountain ridge to speak of, though I knew they were there. The landscape beyond the snow-dredged deck was tenebrous and desolate, but there was a weight to it that was far too heavy to suggest it was barren. It suddenly occurred to me that practically anything could inhabit those 300 acres of shadows. Even impossible things. Things we thought we lost.

In a phantasmic flourish, my mother emerged into that abyss like Jesus in Veronese's famous Resurrection painting. Her eyes were directed upward, and her arms and legs formed a "T." Suspended there in a gulf of nothing, she cocked her head and expectorated rope after rope of red liquid like a spitting cobra. Blood. A laugh came from somewhere, anywhere. Its unnaturalness made me question whether my sense of hearing was a gift or a curse.

I jumped at the squeal of the sliding glass door behind me. It was Delco, hands tucked into his pockets and a cigarette jutting from his mouth. He had the hood of his pullover up, which pushed his shoulder-length hair against his face like two strange mutton chops. I turned back toward the darkness and downed a huge gulp of wine. The illusion was gone. The grief would always be there.

"No need to freak, kid," he said. "It's just me." He shimmied as he rummaged through his pockets for a lighter. "It's colder than a fuckin penguin's balls out here, isn't it?"

"Yep," I replied.

"I left home for warmer weather, and you guys are trying to send me back. Unbelievable."

I didn't even bother with a response this time because I didn't want to encourage him. Delco and I were rarely alone together, and I wanted to keep it that way. I don't think I'd ever seen him sober, and once he started cross-buzzing, he was capable of any crazy old thing. I'd once seen him piss on someone at a football tailgate. But that wasn't the only reason I didn't take to him. He was a handsome guy who made friends with ease, and I suppose, on some level, I was jealous of that.

He fixed his glazed eyes on my cigar. "Stogie?" he questioned. "That's what's up."

I took another drink and a deep breath. "It's pretty decent," I allowed, praying he wouldn't ask the question I knew he was mulling over.

But then he did: "You mind if I hit that thing?"

I fought off a sigh and reluctantly passed it to him. He drew on the torpedo cigar several times only to produce thin, unsatisfying wisps of smoke. Each time he looked at it with confused, furrowed eyebrows like it was a pen that wouldn't write. "You know you didn't cut it right, right?" he said. "The opening is way too small."

I took it back and examined it. "Works all right for me," I replied, puffing a ring in his direction.

The conversation was going downhill fast when the sliding door whistled open yet again. Andy, Freddie, Beau, Mike, and Jake poured onto the porch, several of them nearly skidding from their feet to their asses courtesy of the slick planks below. Each of them held a sideways can of beer, their shoulders arched in the ceremonial posture of shotgunning. They passed around a set of keys, using them to puncture jagged mouthpieces into the base of their cans.

"Gentlemen," Andy announced. "It's a pleasure to be here with y'all this weekend."

Everyone countersigned his statement in their own way. Then they proceeded to turn their cans right-side-up above their heads and pluck the tabs. Within five seconds, it was over, and they spiked their empties to the porch. They leaned there like five stooges, burping and giggling and nudging one another triumphantly. All except for Jake.

"You didn't finish yours, you pussy," he screamed

at Mike, throwing in an accusatory pointer finger for added effect. "You spilled half of it on the ground."

"It's not the destination," Mike said calmly. "It's the journey."

Jake cocked his eyes to the side and drifted into deep thought. I could tell that the numbers weren't quite adding up in his head. "I'm pretty sure what you just said doesn't apply to this scenario, but when I know for a fact, I'll get back to you," he slurred. Then he lumbered back into the house, raised his arms, and hollered, "Ayyy!"

Freddie laughed as he walked over to me and offered a handshake.

I took it. "How've you been, Freddie?" I asked.

"I can't call it," he said, his voice marble smooth.

"You been working on any rhymes?" Delco asked him.

Freddie paused for a second. "I don't rap," he said.

Aside from being a purveyor of random hellhound facts, Freddie was also a ridiculously talented writer of both fiction and nonfiction alike. But no one had taken him seriously because of the color of his skin.

Delco had taken a joint that Mike started. "But you're sick with the words, bro," he said, breathing in. "You should totally rhyme. Just sayin." There was that smirk again as he exhaled, the smoke curling into the rest of the fog and draping over us like a pool of silky, yet poisonous, clouds.

"If you say so," Freddie said.

I pulled on my cigar, bottomed out the rest of my cup.

Chapter Twelve

We sat around the large dinner table playing a drinking game, the clamor of our voices melding with the heavy bass of the background music. Freddie and Livy had turned in early so that they could get up at the crack of dawn to go skiing. Mike and Maggie would be the only other two going, but they had chosen to brave what would surely be a formidable hangover to make the most of the first night at the house.

It was now past midnight, and my head was starting to swim. I guess I shouldn't have been surprised. I'd polished off my bottle of wine in just over an hour, and now I was moving on to beer. I glanced up at the wall behind the head of the table several times; a reproduction of *The Last Supper* loomed there, watchful and judgmental above my half-burned cigar on the antique table below. I decided I didn't trust it. I also decided that I was buzzed.

Danielle drew a card from the deck and read it: "The person who last used the restroom has to take a drink." She looked around expectantly before the lightbulb went off. "Oh no," she lamented dryly. "That was me!" She threw her cup back, slapped it on the table, then pumped a fist at the heavens in one fell swoop. "Damn these cursed cards," she said, splitting the word "cursed" into two syllables. "They're out to ruin me."

Willa laughed so hard she snorted. She beamed at me with that infectious smile she gets when she's tipsy, and I sat my hand on her knee.

Eden took a card from the pile next. "Everyone who is taller than you finishes their drink," she said, covering her thin mouth as she staved off a chuckle.

There was a collective groan. Everyone was taller than Eden. Except for Livy, and she was asleep. We did as the card commanded—which was unfortunate considering I'd just cracked a fresh beer—and then went to the refrigerator or our respective coolers for refills.

"Line o'clock," Delco announced, straddling one of the bar stools. He took a rolled dollar bill and snorted a skinny trail of powder from the counter. His eyes had turned from rheumy to loopy as the night progressed, and I wasn't keen on how zooted he was starting to look. His pupils were now deserted water wells of inebriation.

It's funny how the minutest sensory detail can transport you to another time and place. For me, it was now the ripping sound of insufflated air as Delco ingested whatever the hell it was he ingested. If only for a fleeting moment, I found myself in my bedroom at my mother's house, a coarse stream burning, dripping from my nasal cavity into my throat. My head was leaving me. There was the most insignificant sprinkling of white residue on the desk; it looked like the remnants of an evened-off cup of confectioners' sugar. Some people's demons were buried deep down. Mine were in these ragged mites of dust.

Once we reconvened at the table, all eyes were on a rosy-cheeked Beau, who now found sitting a lot easier than standing. "Everyone wearin a wristwatch drinks," he announced from his card.

That was about half of us, including me. Danielle poked her watchless boyfriend, who now stretched over the table with his head in his arms. Jake peered up, demolished a drink that may or may not have been his, and returned his noggin to his makeshift pillow without so much as a word.

"Why aren't you drinking?" Willa asked Mike.

"Because my watch is not a watch," he said. "It's a phone."

"Shut up, Mike," came from somewhere. From whom, we'll never know.

The game carried on like this for another half hour or so, and the details became increasingly storyboard-like and hazy. One card became the next; one song became the next; one laugh became the next; one roller coaster feeling of euphoria became the next. The pouring of wine or liquor sounded new and foreign as it collided with the sides of plastic cups like miniature waves crashing ashore. Conversations took on new lives and languages of their own. Each trip to the bathroom became more frequent and difficult to maneuver.

At one point, Willa and I looked up to discover Livy in the kitchen, eating a plain tortilla in her pajamas, staring straight ahead like she'd seen a ghost. She was charmingly big-eyed, random, and sneaky, and she had a knack for being funny without trying.

"What are you doing?" Willa asked, laughing before she could even finish the question.

"I am famished," Livy plainly said. Then she scampered off toward her bedroom, nibbling all the while.

From that point forward, the evening devolved into its normal house-party atmosphere. In my head, everything was slow, but the environment around me moved at its normal, worldly pace. I searched the room. Delco was making a pass at Maggie, Andy was canoodling Eden, and Willa and Danielle were catching up on grad school. Beau was successfully articulating about one of every four words in a vigorous conversation with Mike, who looked so crossed that it was a miracle his eyes were still open. Jake breathed in long, labored sighs, absent from this plane of existence.

I drank more and more. It was always like this. I stress-ate in social situations like dinners and work parties, and I did the same thing with drinking when the booze was flowing freely. I was on the verge of losing control when I wisely decided to step outside and look at pictures of Pinto, a move that always seemed to inexplicably reel me back in. But as soon as I was alone in the frigid small hours of the morning, I turned my attention toward the doomful darkness before me instead. It haunted and bewildered me, just as it had before—more so, even.

The words came to me in a whisper: "I'll pray for you." Then they were gone.

I couldn't have been out there for any longer than five minutes before a plastered, new-to-the-world Jake joined me. He threw his arm around me before I could even turn. "Whatcha up to, man?" he asked.

"Just getting some fresh air," I replied, realizing that I was partly holding him up as I did so.

"Close the door, Jake!" someone shouted from inside.

"Swear to God, I'll fight you right now!" he snapped

back. But then his mind switched gears. "You know," he said, struggling to speak, pulling me to one side with him. He might as well have had a yellow "Caution: Words Slippery When Wet" sign around his neck. "Willa brought some other dudes around before you, and I never thought they were cool." He looked at me. "But you're all right."

"I appreciate that," I replied. And I truly did.

Jake looked like he had something else to say, but he didn't. He dropped his arm from my shoulders, back-pedaled two steps, and plopped down into one of the porch chairs. He was snoring in less than a ten count.

I could feel myself smiling for the briefest of moments before I was once again lost in the black horizon beyond the railing. I slipped into it, found myself a creature of it. Both its mysteries and inevitabilities laid flat and bare like a Stygian lake with no wind to stir it. Or perhaps an evil, empty mirror. No matter the numbness the alcohol and the pills afforded me, something still didn't feel right here as I sought the world before me and found no discernable end. All my life I'd been running from something. I just hoped it wasn't going to catch up to me here.

Part 2

Chapter Thirteen

The question came flooding back to me, this time not from the yellow teeth of my mother's former classmate, but rather some far-off place that couldn't be pinpointed: "Was she saved?" It almost sounded like the voice on the hair-raising rendition of "Country Roads, Take Me Home," but it couldn't have been. I was standing over my mother's casket, and the evening quest for Blue Brier wouldn't take place for nearly another three years.

I considered the question all the same as I ran my hand along the silk liner. My mother had accepted Jesus as a little girl at the First Baptist Church on Main Street. I can still see the faded white steeple with the sundial out front. She had been a devout member there until the shedding of her mortal coil some fifty years later. But saved from what? She hadn't been spared the pain of a cruel world and a life that was equally unkind.

She hadn't been exempt from the agony of those final moments. She hadn't been rescued from me. Staring into her sunken face, I somehow doubted that death had liberated her from anything. As far as I was concerned, she would never have the chance to even the score. Where was the salvation in that?

The room began to swim in miragelike waves as I put the back of a shaking hand on my mother's cheek. It felt like paper. I pulled back quickly, dipping my head and fighting off a new phalanx of tears. Then I heard a series of low popping noises that put me in mind of water dripping from a bathtub faucet, infrequent at first but multiplying by the second. I looked up. Slowly, my mother's eyes peeled open until they were full and wide and stock-still in her cranium. Once a lush brown, they were now hoary and glacial. I knew as well as the next person that the body performed involuntary functions after death, but I wasn't fooling myself. My mother was looking at me.

Reality eroded beneath me. I stepped back and tried to scream, but my mouth wouldn't open. That's how I knew I was dreaming. I heard, "Heath, wake up," as though it was coming from inside a car with rolled-up windows. Two or three more of my muffled squalls came to pass before I bucked through the nightmare and shot straight up in bed. I was drenched with a sheet of sweat, licks of hair pasted to the back of my neck, breathing like I had run a marathon. My head was throbbing like a freshly flayed blister. The room was still crowded with the early morning's darkness, and the clock read a quarter of seven.

I was at the house on Mouth of Sheol, and Willa's hands were on my forearm. "Are you all right?" she asked, her voice husky with sleep.

"I'm good," I said. I unpacked a heavy breath.

"Bad dream?"

"The worst."

We opened the door of our bedroom and found that we weren't the first ones up. Freddie, Livy, Mike, and Maggie congregated in the kitchen. Behind them, Beau was working on some eggs and sausage at the stove. He poked at each with a spatula, eyes glued half-open, looking about rode hard and put up wet. We rounded the outdated pullout couch where Delco lay snoring and crooked as a question mark.

"Good morning," Livy said, much too chipper for the hour. She was the definition of a morning person. An early riser. A go-getter.

Willa and I were less enthusiastic in our responses. I think one of us managed a half-hearted flick of the wrist. I headed straight for the coffee pot and checked every cabinet in the kitchen for aspirin.

"How'd y'all sleep?" Livy asked.

"Pretty good," Willa said.

"I've had better nights," I replied.

"Yeah, we heard one of y'all in there screaming," Freddie chuckled. "That was you?"

"That was me," I laughed. "Just chasing away old spooks is all. It's really hot in that room."

"I hate sleepin in a hot room," Beau chimed in from seemingly out of nowhere, eyes still downcast on the sizzling food. "Gives me swamp nuts."

Freddie almost spat out his coffee, and Willa grimaced. Mike and Maggie looked sufficiently tuned-out and hungover.

I heard Livy whisper, "What's swamp nuts?" to Freddie.

"Who's hungry?" Beau asked, holding up a skillet.

The seven of us sat at the big table and ate our breakfast while the other five continued to sleep. Daylight was flowing in at a brisk clip and casting morning shadows every which way in the living room and beyond. The flywheel of the Singer sewing machine stitched jagged webs onto the wall beside it. A thin, blurry layer of condensation blemished the picture window. *The Last Supper*, still somewhat obscured in the dimness, observed us as we all wolfed down our food, and Delco's deviated septum provided the soundtrack to our lazy conversations.

"Is it really only the four of us going?" Livy asked, looking from Maggie to Mike to her boyfriend, Freddie.

"Oh, so we're not enough?" Mike asked.

Livy ignored him—as she had a habit of doing—and glanced at Willa. "I still think y'all should come," she said. "You're missing out."

I didn't know about that. I'd been snowboarding before, and the prospect of busting my ass in front of strangers didn't seem so attractive at twenty-nine. Then there was the issue of the rental fees, of course. Willa was known to call me a fuddy-duddy, and for these reasons, I suppose she was right to do so.

I chewed my food, sipped at my coffee. "We're good. It's an hour away, and we don't really have the money, anyway. I think we'll just stay here and chill."

Willa frowned at me. She hated it when I spoke for her, and I think she was about to say as much when Mike cut in.

"That reminds me," he said. "Can I borrow your truck, Beau?"

Beau speared a chunk of sausage with his fork and glared at Mike like he'd asked the question in a different language. "Come again."

"Can I borrow your truck?"

"Why would you need to borrow my truck?"

"Me and Maggie rode up with Heath and Willa," Mike explained. "And Freddie and Livy are in a two-seater, so there isn't enough room."

Beau thought about it for less than a second. "Uh uh," he said, shaking his head and shoveling scrambled eggs into his mouth.

I could tell that Mike was considering a pivot toward Willa next, but he must have quickly realized that that dog wouldn't hunt. Willa's car was new, and I was lucky to drive it myself.

"Please, Beau?" Maggie said. "I bought snow pants just for this."

He sighed, eyes still red and strained with the previous night's indulgences. "All right," he said, staring a hole into Mike. He held out the key. "But it better be brought back as is or my foot's gonna have a pow-wow with your ass."

Freddie almost lost his coffee again.

Mike looked unaffected except for his hair, which gave the impression that a comb had never touched it. "I'll come back dead before I come back with a scratch on your truck," he assured. He pushed himself away from the table, cautiously grabbed the key from Beau's hand, and went into the bathroom to change.

"I swear that boy's so dumb he could throw himself on the ground and miss," Beau said.

Chapter Fourteen

As soon as the group of four was bound for South-ernmost Ski Resort, I picked up what remained of my cigar and stepped out onto the wraparound porch with Beau. The temperature had continued to plummet throughout the night and was now stabilized in the up-per twenties. It felt pleasant against the pain gnawing away at my temples, against the craving working its way into my every fiber. A sheen of ice stretched across the porch and glinted under a smothered sun that was quick-ly being overcome by grayness in all directions. That bewitching grayness.

I sniffed at the air, hoping the odor of sulfur had diminished, if not disappeared altogether. I was in no such luck.

"Smells like gunpowder out here, don't it?" Beau said, a shiver in his voice.

I nodded, lit my cigar, and brooded at the area ahead. The space behind the railing had been a flat and formless mire of black sky mere hours before, but now it had shape and texture. The expanse of land below the house sprawled a pale and prone yellow over miles of tumbling hills, copses of gaunt trees on either side. At the end of the horizon, dull blue mountains extended left to right for as far as the eye could see. Thick clouds lay over them like giant cloth rollers in the production room of a textile plant. They were as gray as tombstones. This looked like a place where the sun didn't stand a chance.

"Dreary day if I ever seen one," Beau said.

"Yep," I responded. I let the mellow smoke churn in my mouth. "My kind of morning."

Beau toed at a slick spot on the porch and laughed. "I guess you gotta find the Lord in the sun *and* the rain, don't you?"

"I wouldn't know," I said.

"Aw, that's right. You're an atheist, ain't you?"

I ashed the cigar over the rail. "I don't know what I am," I said. "Irreligious would be the best word for it, I guess."

"You a 'Higher Power' kind of person?"

"No, not really," I replied, zoning out.

I didn't understand why at the time, but at that moment, my mind traveled back to the previous summer. Willa and I were sight-seeing in Savannah, Georgia, and we'd taken shelter from an isolated thunderstorm in a large cathedral that looked like it belonged to another place and time. We entered into the rear nave through arched double doors that groaned like old joints and passed the baptismal font under the organ loft, our mouths agape at the sheer size of the sanctuary. Stained glass windows bled various colors of sparse light onto three aisles of old, wooden pews, and walls of painfully detailed murals bookended the altar at the front.

We scooched into a row toward the back, and we

weren't alone. Two dozen or so people looked as if they, too, had come to flee the rain. Half that number seemed to be there actually worshipping. And the cathedral still appeared nearly empty; I remember thinking a few thousand could probably fit in there on a good day. Willa fixed her eyes straight ahead, admiring the high, domed roof of the apse above the altar with its gold rafters and finishes. But I just sat there—dumbfounded—seeing but not seeing.

Rain pattered thickly on the windows, and I was wordless. The beauty of the cathedral was so palpable that it made me ache. But I was melancholic and unmoved—or at least not moved in the way I wanted to be. I couldn't escape the feeling that eventually the rain would find us inside.

I turned to Willa and said, "I'm sorry I'm lost."

That feeling returned to me as I looked over the Mouth of Sheol with Beau at my side. My head was beginning to float from the nicotine buzz I was getting from the cigar. I simply hadn't noticed it the night before because the alcohol had masked it. Now, it was coming for me with a vengeance, and it wasn't doing my headache any favors. My stomach rolled over like Pinto on a lazy Sunday.

Beau mused the landscape. "I was thinkin it'd be nice if we all went on a walk later. Just a little ways out yonder. Would you be up for it?"

I hiccupped a mixture of smoke and the previous night's wine-beer cocktail, then coaxed it back down. "Yeah, I think me and Willa are gonna run into town to get a few things, but I'd be game later on. I guess we don't have anything else to do until we start drinking."

"Solid," Beau said, plugging a fresh gobbet of chewing tobacco between his lip and gums.

We went back inside, where Jake and Danielle were picking over what was left of the cold, greasy breakfast. They looked groggy and languid, like the actors from commercials for prescription sleep medication. Or maybe more like zombies scavenging for putrescent flesh in a field that was slim pickings. Delco shifted behind them and possibly farted, but he didn't wake up.

"Thanks for waiting on us, you assholes," Jake said in our general direction.

"He doesn't mean it," Danielle assured, her eyes glassy and her voice hoarse. "This looks great."

I scanned the room. It looked even more wholesome in the daylight than it had the night before, minus the innumerable beer cans strewn about the tables and countertops. I reckoned a room like that couldn't have been accustomed to hearing such language, and I almost felt dirty and ashamed.

Jake sat down at the table and scowled at his food. Then he ran his pointer finger along the inside of his mouth. "Does your tongue ever feel like a caterpillar?" he asked, eyes turning inward from what surely must have been a no-nonsense headache.

"What are you talking about?" I asked, feeling my facial muscles twisting in confusion.

Danielle didn't even look up. "Jacob Nhem, I love you, but you're an idiot."

"I'll second that," Beau said.

"I'm serious," Jake continued. "Like when you don't brush your teeth after a long night of drinking, and you wake up and it feels fuzzy."

"Why didn't you brush your teeth?" Danielle asked.

"Because we forgot to bring toothpaste."

"Oh shit, you're right," she said, the realization dawning on her.

"Willa and I are gonna run to Blue Brier here in a little bit," I said. "Y'all are welcome to join."

I'd no more than finished my sentence when Willa herself emerged from our bedroom, shaking her head as wet hair corkscrewed about her shoulders.

"What is it?" I asked.

"The air outside isn't the only thing that smells like sulfur. That shower water is like a rotten egg."

Someone responded to her, but I didn't hear it. My mind wandered off to a different place, a stop along the road between déjà vu and premonition. The creepy lady from up the road returned to me with her blank gaze and spectral paleness, the veins on the back of her hands standing up like the roots of a sickly tree. What was it that she had said? "Them people have to fend for themselves in all that sulfur and brimstone." Yeah, that was it.

Brimstone.

And sulfur.

Sulfur. It crawled from her mouth and dissipated, and suddenly it wasn't aloof—it was sinister.

"Heath," Willa said.

I didn't react at first.

"Heath," she repeated.

I snapped out of it.

"Jake and Danielle are gonna go into town with us," she said. "Do you wanna go get changed?"

"Yeah," I stuttered.

I gave my head a stiff shake and rubbed my eyes. Then I inhaled deeply. The rancid scent of sulfur was now strong inside the house.

Chapter Fifteen

We departed the house on Mouth of Sheol Road at a few ticks before nine o'clock, Jake and Danielle in the back of the SUV, Willa and I up front. A skin of fresh frost covered the windshield, just as the bitter taste of a capsule was fresh on my tongue as I descended the one-way gravel road carefully, hoping there would be no incoming traffic to greet me; I didn't want to find out what it was like to have to turn around or move over on such a narrow path.

The surrounding woods, though still bare and spindly, were far less menacing now in the pallid daylight as we approached the decrepit shack from the night before. Its two front windows were like sightless eyes, and its tumbledown porch bowed into a frown above a flowerbed from which nothing grew and a fallow patch of earth that was more like a swidden than a lawn. The wooden-planked roof was eaten alive with dry-rot, and there was no sign of light or movement beneath it. I couldn't fathom anyone calling that place home.

"That's where the crazy lady was," Willa said in a

somber tone. "Just standing there in that yard."

"What yard?" I asked, braking for a moment. "That grass looks torched."

"Damn," Danielle said.

"What crazy lady?" Jake asked.

Willa sighed. "Never mind, Jake."

We trundled on until we reached the first house on the road, the yellow double-wide with the portentous sign on its shed.

PREPARE TO MEET THY GOD

It looked even grimmer in the morning. The black pickup truck was gone, but there was something we hadn't noticed before, too: a weathered red barn that resided in the middle of a clearing a stone's throw behind the house. Its door was cracked, and white shapes flitted from the chasm it created. One head poked out from the right side of the darkness. Then a second from the left. Each belonged to its own droll, bored-looking goat.

"Goats!" Willa shouted delightedly as I braked to a stop.

Their mouths moved in almost imperceptible chewing motions as they watched us from within the barn, eyes dead, perhaps judgmental. They were otherwise still as two logs, ivory-colored and dirty—like the traces of snow left on the ground around us.

"They're so cute and goofy," Danielle said.

"I wish we could go pet them," Willa added.

"I'm not sure they're the petting zoo type," I said, driving on.

The goats continued to watch us with those half-lidded eyes until they were replaced by the tree line in the rearview mirror.

It wasn't long before we reached the four-way intersection at the end of Mouth of Sheol Road. I could see the vast sweep of land on my left and the decaying, weed-surrounded building across the road straight ahead. But I didn't see any indication of the ill-fated coyote we'd left there the night before.

"It's gone," I said.

"What's gone?" Willa asked.

"The coyote."

She looked concerned, but she didn't respond. Not at first. I hung a right onto Yellow Sulfur Springs and traveled a ways down the road before she finally did. "What do you think got it?" she asked.

"Probably whatever got it in the first place," I said, gravely.

We took Yellow Sulfur Springs to the Aylett Mercer Parkway, which displayed a glum, yet gorgeous complexion beyond its guardrails. A mosaic of spiraling trees and pale mountains consumed the landscape. I had seen few sights that rivaled it to that point in time. We passed an outpost that looked like it had nineteenth-century origins; a faded sign in the shape of a smiling Smokey the Bear sat out front. It read:

TODAY'S RISK OF FOREST FIRES IS LOW

There was something strangely comforting about Smokey's noble eyes and confident thumbs up.

I heard Jake mumble, "Ol'-stop-drop-and-roll-lookin-ass."

We soon came upon the residential neighborhoods with their Hellenic-inspired homes and ominous yard signs and followed them to the downtown area. Blue

Brier was quaint and easygoing in the daytime. Cars were parked here and there on the sides of the street, and forgotten Christmas decorations donned the doorways of small businesses. Two old men sat on the stoop of a diner, drinking coffee. There was a church, a laundromat, a daycare we hadn't noticed on the way in. There was a graveyard on a hill, its fifty-some-odd tombstones sloping upward in a rabble of granite.

When I saw the sign that read "General Store & Grocery," I pulled into the parking lot behind it. There was only one other car—an old Jeep Wagoneer with wood side-paneling and a black smudge where an embossed logo used to be. We entered through the back of the building into a dim room that stunk of mildew and a sweetness that I couldn't quite identify. The store was divided into two halves by titled shelving. On one side sat barrels of candy and open cases of homemade goods, like preserves, sauces, and honey. On the other side stretched short aisles of everyday grocery items like bread and nonperishables.

"I'm getting some pizza rolls," Jake announced, tearing off toward the cold case in the back corner with Danielle in tow.

Willa and I browsed the grocery aisles for snacks, our footfalls creaking in the musty stillness, flimsy pillows of dust swirling in the air.

"Do we need to get anything for dinner tonight?" I asked.

"No," Willa said. "Beau bought the ingredients to make spaghetti for everyone. He's very adamant about it."

I laughed. Then I walked to the front of the store to grab a basket, hoping I would see an employee, or at least another customer, but the room was deserted.

I went back to Willa, and she dropped a few items in the basket.

"I'm not entirely sure anybody works here," I told her.

"Then I guess all this stuff is free," she said. She pecked me on the cheek.

Jake and Danielle joined us in the snack aisle, a hodgepodge of items in their arms, including two toothbrushes.

"This place is like something out of a Clint Eastwood movie," Jake said.

"Yes," Danielle replied. "Because I'm sure they had Hot Pockets in the Wild West."

Jake paused. "I'm gonna need you to check the 'tude," he said, a bag of potato chips crinkling between his fingers.

We walked to the front counter, which looked more like a librarian's desk with a misplaced old-timey, manual-input cash register. A display of aerosol cans sat on the opposite side, half the empty, refillable kind, the others full of bear deterrent. The labels of the latter depicted a very cartoonish grizzly with Xs for eyes coughing a cloud of green smoke. On the wall behind the counter, a tin sign claimed:

This Establishment is Protected by God and a Gun.

"Where's the cashier?" Danielle asked.

I began looking for a bell to ring when the whining sound of a door opening and closing issued from somewhere off to the side. A man in a dark-green apron emerged from one of the aisles, rounded the counter, and assumed his position at the register without saying a word. He was nondescript save a long beard the color of a well-spent charcoal briquette.

"Y'all find everything okay?" he asked, plucking at the keypad of his register with gangly fingers, his mouth lost in his beard like a grave marker that has been overcome by moss. His voice was low and calm, but not in a soothing way.

"I think so, yeah," I said.

He rang up a few of the items, then dropped his hands flat on the counter and studied us for a moment or two, the shape of his blue eyes unchanging. I knew the question he was going to ask before he asked it. "Y'all ain't from around here, are you?"

"No, sir," I said. "Is it that obvious?"

"Just ain't seen y'all before, is all," he replied, bagging our coffee. "If you been here for more than five minutes, you can probably tell this is a everybody-knows-everybody-type of town. People born here tend to stay 'til Peter calls their name to the throne for the Judgment."

I tried my best to come off as interested while hoping he would speed things up. But he didn't.

"What brings y'all here?"

"Some of our friends are at Southernmost right now," I said. "We're just relaxing at a house we rented."

"Where y'all from?" he asked.

"North Carolina," Jake said. "Ever been?"

"Cain't say that I have," the merchant replied. He bore this expression like he was doing complicated math in his head. "Naw, I've never been further away than about twenty-five miles in any given direction."

"Really?" Jake asked a little rudely.

Danielle pinched him.

"Yessir. Some people might not think that's the most excitin existence, but on the flip side, I'd say it qualifies me as an expert on the area. So if y'all have

82

any questions about what's what, I reckon I'm your man."

I didn't ask right away, but then I couldn't help myself. "What's this hellhound rumor I've been hearing about? Is that something y'all just tell the out-of-towners?"

His expression turned dour. "Who told y'all about that?"

"A lady a few houses down from ours."

He maintained his stern countenance for a moment or so before switching back to a more light-hearted look. "It ain't a rumor. More of a legend, really." He deposited the last of our items in a paper bag. "But I know people who'll swear by it."

"How so?" I asked.

He tilted his head toward the ceiling. "Well, there's Levon Petrea. Used to be a highway patrolman that worked the stretch from here to Webster Springs. He can tell you the story a lot better'n I can, but I recollect a good bit of it." He wet his lips. "About ten years back, he was up on the Mercer Parkway late one night, and he come upon this drunk just standin there in the middle of the road, shakin and spoutin all kinda nonsense. Said he smelled bad enough to gag a maggot. Well, Levon just reckoned he needed to sleep it off, so he put him in the back of his cruiser and was on his way to the station when the man started carryin on real bad. Sayin, 'He's gonna get me,' over and over, 'He's gonna get me.' Said he was writhin and blubberin like a baby.

"Levon told him to calm down, but when he looked out the windshield ahead, he seen a pair of barn-red eyes dancin there like they weren't attached to no body. Kindly floatin, gettin bigger and bigger. He heard the man gasp the Lord's name right about the time he slammed on the brakes. The red eyes was gone in a flash, but when he turned toward the backseat, so was the man. He wasn't nowhere to be found. Like he was raptured into the sky or somethin. Or maybe to somewhere else." The merchant paused, glanced at the counter. "Levon turned his badge in the next day. He preaches the Gospel over at the Independent Baptist Church now."

I can only imagine how we were looking at him when he finished his story—dumbfounded, skeptical, a little scared.

He smiled for the first time. "I know what you're thinkin, and it's true. Some people around here lie like a no-legged dog. But not Levon. He's about as honest as they come. But I cain't confirm it for myself. That's his testimony." He sat the bags on the counter. "Other people have their own interpretations. Some say 'it,' whatever it is, lives on top of the mountain not too far from here. Some say it hides in the mines to the north."

I thought about the bewitching grayness—the steam rising from the earth. "What do you say?" I asked, my heart rate slightly accelerated.

"Like I told you. That ain't my testimony to give."

The merchant and I stared at each other wordlessly for a handful of breaths before I spoke next. "So this thing—does it prey on just people or other stuff, too?" I imagined the small, piercing eyes of the coyote.

"They say it has a taste for humans, although I don't think a taste is necessarily what it's after. But once it has its sights set on you, that's pretty much all she wrote." He cleared his throat. "Legend says when you look into its eyes, it's worse than your deepest fear. Injuns say a person who's experienced real pain can escape it at first, but it only prolongs the inevitable. It's gonna get you eventually."

"Don't you mean Native Americans?" Willa asked.

The man chuckled. "If you say so."

The jingle of the front door interrupted our deteriorating conversation. In strolled a snake-hipped old man with a straw horseman's hat. He sported black cowboy boots and a pair of Wrangler blue jeans, both well-worn, and a gray t-shirt that said:

My Savior is Tougher than Nails

A badge was pinned there on the left side of his chest. He struck me as the type of man you'd expect to have a thick mustache, but there was no mustache. There was barely any hair at all. He moseyed over to the counter.

"Sheriff," the merchant said.

"Howboutya, Jasper?" the old man replied, voice squeaking like car brakes in the rain. He smiled. His teeth were too straight and white to be anything other than dentures. He turned his attention toward me and held out his hand. "Sheriff Jimmie Wimmens."

I took it reluctantly. "Heath." I motioned behind me. "My girlfriend, Willa. My friends, Danielle and Jake."

"Pleasure," he said, tipping his hat.

"They're from North Carolina, Sheriff," the merchant chimed in, a hint of mockery in his tone.

Jimmie Wimmens propped his elbow on the counter. "Aw, whereabouts?"

"Durham," I said.

He adjusted his hat. "That's quite a change of pace from here if my memory serves me correct. Y'all are probably lost without the gluten-free aisle and the self-checkout lane."

The merchant snickered.

"We're making do," Willa said.

Jimmie Wimmens hoicked his eyebrows—what little eyebrows he had. "Glad to hear it." He thumbed the brim of his hat. "Well, we got us a nice little setup around here. Real quiet, real Christian. You shouldn't have any trouble, but if y'all need anything, just gimme a holler. We're over at the magistrate's office."

"The one with the Confederate statue?" Willa asked. She wasn't missing a beat.

"That's the one." He turned toward the merchant. "Jasper, I'm gonna go over yonder and grab some hard candy for the missus. I'll be back up in a jiff." He shot us one last look and tipped his hat. "Y'all take care now."

"Forty-six, nineteen," the merchant said in that stolid voice as the sheriff bumbled off.

"I'm sorry?" I replied.

"The groceries. Forty-six dollars and nineteen cents."

"Y'all can just pay me back," I said to Jake and Danielle, reaching for my wallet with a shaky hand.

When we returned to the SUV, we sat in silence like people who don't know each other.

Danielle broke the seal. "Anybody know what the hell that was all about?"

Jake was swiping at his phone with his pointer finger. "I read something on Reddit about a hellhound urban legend, but that happened closer to home. Asheville, I think. A girl was found dragged out of her car with claw marks on her." He paused, squinted at his screen. "Just kidding, it happened in West Virginia, but I'm sure it was on the other side or something." Another pause. "Just kidding, it happened like an hour away from here."

"Fantastic," Danielle said.

"What difference does it make?" Jake laughed. "It's all bullshit. That hayseed was just trying to scare us. He knows we're not from the area." He turned toward the window. "And what the fuck kind of name is Jimmie Wimmens?"

"I don't know," Danielle started, "but that whole conversation just gave me the heebie-jeebies."

"Now y'all know how we felt on the drive last night," Willa said.

Chapter Sixteen

We returned to the house on Mouth of Sheol to find the rest of the gang up and moving around. My drug-abetted, razor-sharp focus zeroed in on Delco, who was over at the counter sniffling and measuring out some lines with a credit card. He offered me a limp, shit-eating grin, eyes spacey and waxed-over. Andy and Eden huddled at the table, giggling over a large bag packed with unidentified brown squares.

"What's so funny?" I asked.

Andy held up the bag, and I could see that it was full of pot brownies. "Want one? We're all gonna do it."

"I'll pass," I said in front of a shy laugh. "I don't do brownies unless I know that I'm five minutes away from a hospital."

"Fair enough," he said, biting the corner of one.

Beau entered the room from the downstairs area, slurping at a beer can. He grabbed a brownie of his own with his mitt of a right hand. "Y'all about ready to roll out?"

"Hell yeah," Delco said. "Let's go build a civilization and never come back." He laughed until his voice was no longer audible.

"How many did you eat?" Willa asked him.

He got himself together, dabbed the corners of his eyes. "I dunno. Three or four."

"Jesus," Danielle said.

We threw on our thicker coats and knit hats, stepped through the house's side door, and descended the wrap-around porch steps into the yard. We headed due east toward a line of trees at Beau's command, eight-across, our feet squishing on the mud beneath the brittle, winter-ravaged grass. Noontime was creeping slow and obligatory through the anemic sky, and a mist was wrapping its arms around the cold air. Acres and acres of land unraveled before us like wet, yellow carpet.

"They must be hitting the slopes about now," I said, thinking about the party of four that cut out earlier.

"Yeah, everybody except for Freddie," Delco said. He had found a massive walking stick somewhere.

"Why do you say that?" I asked.

"Come on, dude," he laughed, spearing that walking stick into the ground with every step. "Black people don't ski."

Willa beat me to the punch. "Yes, they do, Delco."

"Woah, woah, relax," he said. "It was just a joke."

"Well, it wasn't funny," she replied.

Delco backed off, and for a moment, you could cut through the silence like a hot fork through cheesecake. I squeezed Willa's hand affectionately.

Jake cracked the ring tab on a beer as we neared the trees. Through the breaks between them, we could see a downhill clearing with a small body of water directly behind it. It must have been a half-mile away.

"Y'all wanna check it out?" Beau asked.

Everyone agreed, but I was hesitant. "Didn't you say the owner warned you about bears?" I pointed through the trees. "Wouldn't that little pond be a water source?"

"Yeah, but they're just black bears," Beau assured. "Might as well be Winnie the Pooh. They should be hibernating now anyway."

"All right," I said skeptically.

We waded into the trees and found ourselves in a maze of bent branches and rawboned trunks amidst a floor of dead, mushy leaves. Each careful step plunged our boots about half a foot into the muck, and we could feel the roots at the bottom as we plowed ahead. If any animals were around, they were well-hidden.

We carried on until we got about halfway through. That's when we stumbled upon what looked like a fence that ran through the middle of the woods. It was flimsy and made of wire and stood about four feet tall. I remember thinking it wouldn't discourage a chicken. It looked as though something had already made a dent in it as it was.

Beau began to throw a leg over the section that bulged.

"I don't know about this, y'all," I said.

"Why?" Beau asked.

"That's a fence. It's clearly trying to keep something out. Or in."

Beau finished clearing it. "I really don't think we have anything to worry about, Heath."

"Yeah, stop sweatin it," Delco added.

Willa threw me a look like I was embarrassing her.

Eden spoke up. "They're black bears; they're not violent. They'd probably be scared of us and run away if we even saw them."

I shut up and averted my eyes.

"Come on, y'all," Beau beckoned.

Willa and I were the last ones over. Once we started moving forward again, I glanced at her. "I'm glad everyone here is a nature expert," I mumbled.

She pinched me.

The second half of the wooded area was much the same as the first. After we wended our way through the rest of it, we came upon a peaky yellow decline that sloped downward toward the pond. We descended it leisurely, the mountains looming miles ahead of us on the fringe of the firmament.

"You must be really spooked by bears," Beau said, sipping his beer. "Is that your greatest fear or somethin?"

"Hardly," I responded.

"My greatest fear is an alien invasion," Delco butted in. He shuddered.

"Mine is spiders," Beau said. "I don't fuck with that. Seen that video on Twitter of the plate-sized tarantula that carried away that possum. Didn't sleep for weeks."

"I'm right there with you, man," Andy agreed.

"Heights," Willa said.

"Failure," Eden added.

Beau nodded at me. "You never said what yours was, Heath."

I heard the general store merchant's voice in my ears, measured as a hypnotist: "Legend says when you look into its eyes, it's worse than your deepest fear."

I thought up a lie real quick. "The end of the world," I said. It was halfway true. For years, I'd operated with this unavoidable feeling of impending doom. I was always encumbered by a certain degree of existential dread. But it wasn't my greatest fear. That had already been realized.

"Anybody scared of the Mothman?" Beau said.

"What's the Mothman?" I asked.

"Y'all really haven't heard of it?"

Nobody said anything.

"I'm surprised. It was this big, bug-lookin man with ten-foot batwings and red eyes the size of bicycle reflectors. Some kinda alien or nuclear experiment gone wrong. In the late sixties, a couple of gravediggers in Point Pleasant, West Virginia, claimed to've seen it fly over them. Then a few folks drivin by the site of an old WWII munitions plant not far from that.

"There were more sightings, all of them in the same area, but I cain't remember the details." He swallowed. "Well, anyway, about a year later, the town bridge collapsed and killed a whole mess of people. Some of the witnesses said they seen the Mothman standin on it minutes before it happened. I seen a documentary about it. Wild shit. Makes for a good campfire story, at least."

"Damn," Danielle said. "Is that close to here?"

"Naw," Beau answered. "It's about three hours north. I got my doubts, of course."

"Well, you can keep that shit," I said. "I've had my fill of urban legends for the day."

"I dunno," Delco commented. "The world's a huge, crazy place. There's tons of shit we don't know about and never *will* know about. Who's to say what's legend and what's fact?"

For once, I agreed with him.

We surrounded the pond. It was black and murky, and tiny boats of yellow film skated atop it. The temperature wasn't low enough to freeze it, but I still didn't want to think about how cold it probably was. There was a rinky-dink landing that extended about six or seven feet over it, but I wasn't about to try my luck on that. Beau and Delco didn't mind, though. They dashed onto it and gazed out across the water. Andy and Eden plopped down onto the ground next to us, and Jake and Danielle stood there, admiring the mountains. Andy grinned, and Eden began to giggle uncontrollably. It seemed like those brownies were starting to kick in.

"Hey, Danielle," Eden said in an inflection that had almost gone baritone. "What was your greatest fear?" She snorted. "We didn't get to you."

Danielle blushed. "It's kind of embarrassing."

"Nonsense," Andy said. His neatly-coiffed hair parted in the wind. "Let's hear it."

"Mascots," Danielle answered, one notch above a whisper.

"Mascots?" Eden blurted.

"Yeah. Like at sporting events and Disneyland and stuff. I don't know what it is, but I just can't be around them. They scare the living shit out of me. Have since I was a kid."

Eden cupped her mouth and brayed, her eyelids squeezed tight. She leaned backward until she was flat and her chest agitated with laughter.

Danielle and Willa smiled through puzzled faces.

"I'm gonna have to take this one back inside soon," Andy said. "This is clearly her first—and maybe last—time doing brownies."

I joined in the joke to mask what lay at the forefront of my mind. I thought about hellhounds and mothmen—the similarities between the two. The red eyes. The red lights on the side of the Blue Ridge Mountains. I thought about bears. Eden had said they would probably run off if they saw us and we saw them. But what if they had already seen us? What if they were just watching us from afar, stalking in the shadows, waiting for the right moment?

I looked to my right, trying to think about something else. Then the hair stood up on the back of my neck. "Oh, fuck."

94

Chapter Seventeen

It took a moment for everyone to catch up to what I saw, but when they did, the horror was almost tangible. It hung in the air, clung to our clothes like the surrounding mist. There was a thicket about a hundred yards to the left of the pond, and nestled at the edge of it stood a mother black bear with her two cubs, staring at us. One of the babies lay at its mother's feet, and the other stood on its hind legs next to its sibling. They couldn't have been much smaller than Pinto. The mother herself was fat and crouched, her close-together eyes beating down on us like black stars. She must have been pushing four hundred pounds.

"I'll be dipped in shit," Beau said. He and Delco had made their way back toward us. "What do we do?"

Willa slowly slid behind me, and I withdrew my knife from my pocket, though I had no delusions about what good that would do. "I don't know," I said, whispers strained by terror. "I'm not the resident authority on bears."

From the corner of my eye, I could see Delco considering his walking stick. Doing the math on how effective it would be as a weapon. He didn't seem too confident. He also looked really high.

The animals remained as still as the dwindling minutes before a heavy snow.

"I don't understand," Andy said. "Why aren't they hibernating?"

"They're um—they're torporing," Jake replied. The temperature hovered around freezing, but he was glistening with sweat.

"Torporing?"

"It's like hibernation, but they're sleeping for shorter periods of time."

"Now, how in the hell do you know that?" I asked.

"I don't know, I saw it on a fucking nature show."

For a tick or two, there was only the stirring wind in the matted yellow grass. I recalled a documentary I'd seen in a film studies class about a troubled man who lived among Kodiak bears in Alaska until they turned on him and ate him alive while his camera was still rolling. His screams seemed to come to me from some bizarre, hellish universe of torture that had yet to be charted.

Eden let go of a careful breath. "If we posture up and act big and loud, we should be able to drive them away."

"I think that might be the case if she were alone," I said. My eyes danced from Cub One to Cub Two. They were cute little boogers, but they might as well have been Satan's imps in that moment. "But she's got baggage. And something tells me she'll protect it at all costs."

She seemed stumped by that.

"There's a lot of ways I coulda seen myself dying," Delco started, "but I gotta be honest, this wasn't one of them." He sounded on the verge of crying.

"Nobody's gonna die," Beau assured, a beer can cocked and ready to launch in his hand. "But we cain't just stand here and have a starin competition with her. We're scared shitless, but probably not as much as them."

"I don't know," Jake said. "I'm pretty fucking scared."

He had barely finished his sentence when our nightmares began to play out in real-time. The mother bear lumbered forward about ten to fifteen yards, shoulders rolling beneath her fleecy black coat. Even from this distance, her claws fell in heavy thuds as her hesitant cubs scampered along behind her. She came to a slow stop on her haunches in a baleful position, and I could make out more of her monstrous features. She had a squarish frame, a bloated belly, round ears, and a pointed, weather-silvered muzzle. And how could I forget those beady, sunken eyes?

"We're fucked," Jake said.

I think Danielle was praying.

Survival Mode kicked in. "Whatever we do, we can't disperse," I said. "I'll bet she could easily run us down, and we've got a better chance if we stick together."

The mother bear started to pant, her long, pink tongue flicking from her mouth. Then she rose up on her back half and slammed to the ground again with her two front legs closer together, almost as if she were clapping her hands. Willa death-gripped my arm, and I heard gasps from behind me. The mother bear scraped her foreclaws on the grass and charged forward, fur rippling, snout wrinkling in gruesome grooves. She traveled ten yards, twenty, growing bigger all the while, and as soon as she had closed half the distance, she planted and belted a throaty, wheezing roar that sounded like an engine revving in Neutral. Her four sicklelike canines glowed a dingy yellow.

"Godmotherfuckingdammit," Beau screamed.

Others joined in.

My heart skipped a beat.

The bear pounced at the ground again and groaned, a low-pitched, guttural noise. But she didn't move any closer. We all backtracked a few feet, fighting our urge to make a run for it. It was a move that very well may have saved our lives at the time. The mother bear snarled, raked her foreclaws. Then after ridding herself of a few more husky grumbles, she wheeled around and began to amble back toward her cubs. She shot us ma- levolent glances over her shoulder every few paces or so but continued to roam off until she reunited with her young. Once she reached them, she nudged them with her muzzle. The family of three retreated into the trees, and it looked as though they were moving deeper into the woods.

I swung around, dropped my knife, and fixed my hands firmly on my knees, chewing back the puke in my throat. I didn't even want to imagine how I would have felt had I eaten a brownie. Beau still had his beer cocked. Delco held his walking stick like a baseball bat, his chest expanding and shrinking in rapid succession. Jake held Danielle, who sobbed into his shirt, and Andy and Eden just stared ahead like they'd been momentarily scared sober by a poltergeist. I picked up my knife; I hadn't even unfolded the blade.

We collected ourselves and embarked for the house, Andy and I pulling up the rear and walking backward, our eyes never leaving that haggard stretch of thicket.

"I'm not stepping one foot off that porch for the rest of our time here," Eden said once the house was in sight.

"You ain't lyin," Beau agreed. "It'd be a miracle if I didn't shit myself."

Willa walked shoulder to shoulder with me. "Well," she started, her focus on that yellow house superimposed over the gray sky. "One thing you can't say about this trip is that it's been boring."

I lifted her trembling hand to my mouth and kissed the back of it.

Nobody said anything else until we were almost back to the house. Then Jake did. "You know how y'all were all just talking about your greatest fears back there?" He paused. "That was mine."

We laughed. That was all we could do.

Chapter Eighteen

A pitter-patter of rain began its soft march on the house's windows as soon as we were through the door. We gathered in the living room, looking more like a group therapy session than eight friends on vacation. I massaged my eyes and thought about the newest omen in a long list of them. My head was still pounding, and my stomach was doing somersaults.

The only one of us who hadn't taken a seat was Delco. He was pacing back and forth around the kitchen, eyes basted bloodshot red, pupils dilated. "I'm too zonked to deal with this shit right now," he said.

Beau walked over and patted him on the shoulder. "Just chill, man."

"Nah, I'm buggin," Delco said, jerking away. "I gotta get outta here."

"Get outta here?" Beau asked. "Where the hell you think you're gonna go?"

"I don't know, but I can't sit still. I might take a walk."

"Out there?" Beau said in a raised voice, his usually

100

dozy face now flabbergasted. "After what we just ran into?"

Delco flipped his hood, and it collected his hair at the cheeks. "Relax. I'm gonna walk in the opposite direction of their territory, away from the trees." He pocketed a pack of cigarettes, exited through the sliding door, and slipped around the corner of the porch before anyone else could advise him otherwise.

Beau dropped his arms in one clumsy, baffled motion.

"Yeah, that really psyched us out, too," Andy said from the leather loveseat, his somber expression aging him ten years. He patted Eden on the thigh. She looked too stoned to talk. "I think we're gonna go lie down for a while and sober up." The two of them rose and retired into their indirectly lit bedroom and shut the door.

The remaining five of us didn't do anything immediately; we just moped around for the better part of half an hour, listening to the tranquil rhythm of the rain as it graywashed the room. But then Beau, having polished off his second beer since returning to the house, moseyed over to the entertainment center and opened the cabinet to the right of the television. He rummaged through a stack of board games, pulled out a one-thousand-piece puzzle, and sat with his legs crisscrossed in front of the coffee table. Danielle and Willa joined him. Jake heated up some pizza rolls in the microwave.

Feeling overwhelmed, I snuck off to the bathroom. Once I had the door locked behind me, I dealt two tiny, white anxiety pills to the counter space between the his-and-hers sinks, the shakiness of my hand causing them to skitter a few inches before they came to a rest. I breathed. My thoughts strayed into a spasm of light where only my mother's corpse existed. And then, clear as day, I saw her in the mirror next to me. A face, clown-like in its whiteness, with intricate bleeding patterns. Blood trickled through the gaps in her gritted teeth, and she squealed: *What kind of man are you?*

She lifted a curved object and began to lick it clean. It was a human rib bone.

I jolted backward with such force that I nearly lost my footing. I caught myself against the wall behind me and looked down to make sure that my feet were firmly rooted on the floor. When I faced the mirror again, my dead mother wasn't there.

The only thing that mattered now was the task at hand. I pulverized the pills with the bottom of the bottle. Taking them by mouth wouldn't work fast enough. Not this time. So I rolled a dollar bill into a tight tube, arranged the powder with my driver's license, and snorted it in one fell swoop. I welcomed the coarse heaviness in my sinuses as I tilted my head back and raked my face with some water from the sink. I looked into the mirror. Relief was on its way.

I flushed the toilet to avoid suspicion, checked the mirror one more time, and returned to my rightful place on the pullout couch, which was still disheveled from Delco's tossing and turning the night before.

"You okay?" Willa asked.

"Yeah," I said.

The Doors, Fleetwood Mac, and more serenaded us from the loudspeaker as Danielle, Willa, and Beau took their sweet time to fit the pieces of the puzzle together. It was slowly becoming a scene of cuddly, mischievous puppies ransacking a laundry basket.

Time dragged on. The weather outside was perfect for sleeping, and so that's exactly what Jake did on the futon to my right. He dozed with an empty plate on his chest. I couldn't get a wink, though. Instead, with "Riders on the Storm" whirring in the background, I panned the room and realized that the house had more religious overtones than I had noticed at first. Many more. There were bundles of Christian DVDs. There was a hanging wooden sign that read:

AS FOR ME AND MY HOUSE, WE WILL SERVE THE LORD.

There was *Apples to Apples*, but it was the Bible Edition. In the kitchen, there were hand towels with verses of scripture on them. And, of course, there was the reprint of *The Last Supper*, depicting the reaction of Christ's disciples after he announced that one of them would betray him.

A different time and place slinked into my conscience, and I found myself as a little boy on a pew at the First Baptist Church:

It was an evening service. The exact date was unclear, but I must have been ten or eleven. My mother dragged me out here every so often until I reached high school, yet she was nowhere to be found. I could tell by the failing daylight that it was late fall, but the sanctuary was stuffy and hot—as hot as the bedroom in the Mouth of Sheol house. Maybe hotter. The preacher, a towering middle-aged man with an insipid voice, was carrying on about the Last Days.

It was always The Last Days.

The congregation faced the front in tense, hunched positions as if they were onboard a plane and bracing for a crash landing. The preacher was discussing the parallelism between Sodom and Gomorrah and the modern United States, which felt like something he would have done. But then something happened that didn't seem like it came from a memory at all; it seemed like it came from a nightmare. Several members of the congregation wheeled around in their pews and looked at me. Their bodies were human, but their faces were blank canvases. It was as though their heads were wrapped in burlap sacks.

Their words came as bubbling, drowning gasps for breath.

"Jesus is coming," one of them claimed.

"Are you ready?" another asked.

"Turn from thy wicked ways," the last one said.

My bottom lip was quivering, but I couldn't holler.

Then the most horrific display unfolded before my eyes. The preacher doubled over the pulpit, writhing and mewling, his white knuckles sprouting mangy black hair, his clothes ripping into tatters at the seams. Face slathered in sweat, he gazed over the unaffected congregation with shut eyes, and his nose and mouth began to elongate into a shriveled snout with protruding, thorn-like teeth, and the sound of the transformation riddled my skin with gooseflesh. The preacher opened his eyes, and they were full-red in their sockets. I expected him to roar, but he didn't. He laughed. He laughed a laugh that was so thunderous and echoing that it could only have come from the deepest, darkest, emptiest reaches of the planet.

I covered my ears, closed my eyes. I rocked back and forth until I could no longer hear that demonic guffaw. When I dared to open my eyes again, things were back to normal. The preacher, well-kempt as he always had been, uttered a sentence in his banal voice, and something in my mind told me that he really had said this in real life in the First Baptist Church when I was ten or eleven years old. But I couldn't remember what it was. Maybe I had repressed it. Maybe my mind had hidden it as a self-defense mechanism. Perhaps it had simply been washed away by the years of drugs and alcohol. Regardless, it was lost on me now.

Another voice broke my concentration and jerked me back into the present. It was Beau's.

"Has anyone heard anything from our friends?" he asked.

"Livy just texted me," Willa said, studying a puzzle piece. "They should be heading back in an hour or so."

"I hope they get back before too late," Beau replied. "I'm liable to starve, and I ain't startin dinner before they're here." He turned toward me. "You all right, Heath? You look like you seen a haint."

"I'm good," I said.

The doorbell rang. We all looked at each other in a momentary state of paralysis. Like underage kids trying to conduct a secret dorm room party. The sonorous chime came again, longer this time. Beau scrambled to the kitchen bar and began scraping as much as he could into a trashcan. I sprang up, grabbed Delco's bag of weed, and hid it in the drawer of utensils. Danielle killed the music. Willa and Jake stood where they were, unsure of what to do, perhaps thinking we could fool whoever was at the door into believing nobody was home. The doorbell played a third tune, its pitch more drawn out than ever.

"Maybe it's Mike and Maggie," Willa said. "Maybe they left before Freddie and Livy. Maybe we accidentally locked the door, and they can't get back in."

"What if it's the owner?" Jake added.

"I'll go check it out," Beau said, disappearing into

the front bedroom.

"I'll bet it's Delco," Danielle guessed.

We heard murmurs and glanced at each other anxiously. There was the muffled *thud* of a door closing.

Beau reappeared seconds later, not with Mike or Maggie, but with a pallid, nearly hairless man in a straw hat. It was Sheriff Jimmie Wimmens. His cowboy boots clacked on the floor, and he tugged at his belt as he came to a stop.

"Howboutya," he said in that rattish voice, crow's feet bunching about his temples.

"Y'all, this is Sheriff Wimmens," Beau announced.

"We've met," I replied.

"Nice to see y'all again," Jimmie Wimmens said, tipping his hat at Willa and Danielle. "Hope you're enjoyin our little piece of Heaven."

"What's this about?" I asked.

He perused the room with intense eyes like he hadn't heard me. It was as if he'd picked up a scent and was close to finding it. There was something about his mouth, the way the crinkled corners of it coiled up into a permanent smile that didn't seem voluntary.

"Sheriff?"

He puckered his lips and licked them. "Neighbor down the road phoned in a complaint about some noise." He framed it almost like a question.

"What noise?"

"I'd imagine it come from that," he responded, gesturing toward the speaker.

"But Sheriff, we weren't even playin music that loud," Beau assured.

Jimmie Wimmens still wouldn't make eye contact with any of us. Instead, he buried his hands into his back pockets and said, "You'd be surprised how sound carries

106

out here."

He was full of shit, and I knew it. The volume from the music the night before had been much higher. Where had he been then?

Beau sighed. "I'm sorry, sir. We'll try to keep it down."

The sheriff browsed the contents of the kitchen without accepting the apology one way or the other.

"Is there anything else we can help you with?" I asked.

His eyes bounced from tables to counters, then he nodded and chuckled. "Y'all sure are doin some serious beer-drinkin out here, ain't you? Liquor, wine, the whole shebang."

"That's not illegal out here, is it?" I questioned. I could feel my tone becoming more discourteous by the syllable. My mother had told me once that I suffered from not knowing when to shut up.

"Naw," Jimmie Wimmens said, almost pensively. "It bemoans me to say that it ain't. But soon folks'll be restin up for church in the mornin, and all that carryin on can be a mean distraction, if you catch my drift. So I'd kindly appreciate it if you'd keep it down." He pulled out a sucker from his back right pocket—the kind you get at the gas station for a quarter—and unwrapped it before popping it into his mouth. "Y'all are more than welcome to drop by for the early mornin service on your way out, by the way. It's right beside the Laundry. Cain't miss it."

"We'll keep that in mind," Danielle said, her voice careful and faint and devoid of its vintage humor.

Jimmie Wimmens stole another long, hard look, his shadow puddling at his feet. "All right, then. Y'all take care. You know where to find me if you need me."

He pinched his hat. And then he was gone.

The door to Andy and Eden's room was still closed. Delco was still AWOL. Our friends would be coming back from Southernmost Ski Resort soon, but in the mean-time, we were just five people in an unfamiliar place, waiting for the prank show's cameras to show themselves.

"Jimmie fucking Wimmens," Jake said.

"Y'all done upset that Looney Tune down the road so much she called the law on us," Beau laughed.

"There was no way that music was loud enough," I replied. "I don't care what he said. That lady's house is a good two miles down the road."

Beau shrugged and returned to the puzzle. There were still plenty of missing pieces. Danielle and Willa rejoined him. Their faces were stoic, but I could tell they were bothered. It was hard not to be. Jake poured himself a stiff drink, looked at me, and shook his head. I resumed my spot on the couch. And then it came to me in the funny way that all elusive memories eventually come—randomly yet perfectly-timed. I recalled the mystery sentence the preacher at the First Baptist Church had said two decades before. It was from the book of Amos:

"Therefore thus, I will do unto thee, O Israel: and because I will do this unto thee, prepare to meet thy God, O Israel."

Prepare to meet thy God.

Chapter Nineteen

It was a minute or two shy of six o'clock when Freddie and Livy got back. The one thousand-piece puppy puzzle was complete on the coffee table in front of the entertainment center. Jake and Danielle were scrolling their phones apathetically, and Willa and I were thumbing through various magazines. Beau nursed a beer at the dinner table, alone, likely worried about Delco, who was still out there—now in the dark.

Freddie and Livy came in smiling, but that changed as soon as they took one look at us.

"Who up and killed the buzz in here?" Freddie asked.

"You don't even wanna know," Beau answered, his back turned away.

"It's been a weird day," Willa admitted. "Did y'all have fun?"

Livy lit up in that big way she had about her, even though she couldn't have been more than five feet tall. "Yeah, it was awesome. We spent almost the whole day on the black diamonds. Then it started to rain." She reined her excitement back in. "Where's Andy and Eden?"

"Asleep."

"Asleep?"

"Eden ate her first brownie."

"Shit," Freddie laughed. "We might not see her until the morning, then." He searched the room. "What about Delco?"

"It's a long story," Beau said in his best Eeyore impression, still facing the sliding glass door. "We went out for a walk down yonder and come upon a mama black bear and her two cubs."

Livy's eyes grew twice in size, and Freddie followed suit.

Beau continued: "Looked like she was fixin to give us the business at first, but then she pulled back and balked at us. Her and her cubs went deeper into the woods away from us. She was bluffin. I reckon she was tryin to scare us, and it worked." He drank his beer. "Freaked Delco out so bad he had to take a hike in the other direction to get his shit together. He's been out there for hours, and I know he's gotta be geeked out of his gourd. He ate five times as many brownies as everyone else."

I relived that moment in pulsing flashes. Those trundling black shoulders like the gears of some machine gone haywire. That soot-colored muzzle curling over yellow teeth designed to tear skin and sinew and splinter bone. Those eyes. Knowing. Primal. Protective. Complicit in nature's beautiful fury. I don't know why Delco would have wanted to go out there. That would have been the last place I wanted to go.

"Goddamn," Freddie said to Beau. "Should we go look for him?"

Beau traced the top of his can. "Naw. He'll turn up soon enough. He always does." But I don't know if he believed it. It didn't occur to me then, but I think he was so concerned about Delco that he'd forgotten Mike was still out with his truck.

"Have y'all seen Mike and Maggie?" Danielle asked Livy.

"They were with us almost the whole day, except for our late lunch toward the end," she said. "We passed them on our way out. They didn't look like they were in any hurry to get back."

At about that time, Willa handed me her phone discreetly. The text on the screen was from Mike, and it read: **Stopped to hook up. Don't tell Beau.** Mike had signed his name at the end like it was a letter. Of course, he had.

I gave her the phone back, shook my head. I guess it was only a matter of time.

Freddie and Livy left to take showers and change out of their ski wear. Everyone else—except for me— started drinking. The hour of gloaming arrived all at once, and while there was no longer rain, there were no stars, either. Full dark manifested itself as cavernous hands, squeezing the last of the light from the day, spreading fingers of frost across the windows of the yellow mountain house. The stillness was both comfortable and disconcerting.

"Are you gonna drink tonight?" Willa asked me.

I winced. Even the question made me feel a little ill. "I don't know," I said. "I'm still pretty hungover."

"Okay," she replied, a hand on my back. She was my one buoy of peace in a vast ocean of chaos, refusing to be upturned or swallowed by the malicious ebbs and flows. I couldn't imagine losing her out there in all that quiet madness.

"I love you," I said.

Willa kissed me on the cheek. And I didn't drink. Truth be told, I'd never drink again. But that didn't stop the others. As soon as Freddie and Livy returned, everyone fired back a double shot of vodka. Even Beau took a break from his post to join the festivities. They were all still wearing their grimaces and nipping at their chasers when the sliding door opened.

Delco wobbled in, hood half on, wet and dumb-struck. He palmed the dinner table feebly and turned to look at us. His eyes were lacquered with a red, mucoid sheen, and his cheeks were crusted over. Like he'd done a lot of crying. It was the most vacant gaze I had ever seen. I had taken plenty of downers in my time, but I would have been dead before being able to recreate that expression.

Beau rushed over to him. "You all right, man?"

He didn't say anything back.

"Delco," Beau said, snapping his fingers in front of Delco's face. "You all right?" he repeated. "We was worried sick about you. I thought you was bear shit by now for sure."

Delco gaped ahead.

Beau waved his hand and reported back to us, "He's fuckin zooted." He reached into the chest pocket of Delco's pullover and turned up what appeared to be a prescription bottle. He frowned. "Codeine." He gave Delco a playful smack on the cheek. "Dumbass."

"Is he gonna be good?" Freddie asked.

"Yeah," Beau replied.

"He doesn't *look* good," Livy said.

"He's fine," Beau assured. "Help me get him down-stairs."

We trailed Beau and Delco—who was able to go mostly under his own power—down the basement stairs. Beau unhooked Delco's arm from his neck and unloaded him onto the sectional sofa, where he lay flat on his back like a victim of sleep paralysis.

"Should we get him help?" Willa asked.

"Naw, he's just fucked up," Beau answered without hesitation. "I've seen him in worse shape."

"Me, too," Jake said.

"Really, I can drive," I interjected. "I haven't been drinking."

"Let's just give him a while and see," Beau said, a hint of agitation in his drawl. "He'll come around. Between the brownies, the pills, and God knows what else, we need to just let him shake it off. Cain't nothin help him now but time."

That didn't sit well with most of us, but the logistics were grim. It was anyone's guess how far the nearest hospital was, and Delco *did* have a tolerance that seemed to defy science. This wasn't normal, though. There was something in his eyes. Something beyond stoned. It was as if they were filled with this malevolent magic that didn't originate or exist above ground. They weren't moistened with intraocular fluid, but rather a viscous, drool-like liquid.

"We could at least get him out of those wet clothes," Livy said.

Beau scoffed. "He's a grown-ass man, I ain't changin him." He strolled over to the fireplace and started the gas logs.

"That should warm him up," Jake said.

We all nodded in agreement, if only to make ourselves feel better.

"Welp," Beau blurted, clapping his palms together.

"I can go fix supper now that I know he's safe."

Safe. I almost laughed at the usage of the word.

We switched off the basement lights and scaled the steps into the living room. It took more than half an hour, several beers, and multiple good-natured insults from Jake for the mood to lighten. Willa, Jake, Danielle, and me played a few low-stakes games of *Uno* as Beau toiled feverishly over his mawmaw's spaghetti recipe. Freddie whipped up a salad, and Livy prepared garlic bread. The aroma would have been mouth-watering on most occasions, but my stomach was in knots—understandably so.

Beau glanced up from his stirring, an epiphanic expression growing on his face. "Where's Mike and Maggie?"

Willa and I exchanged a look. She said, "They just texted me they'd be back soon, but to not wait for them to eat."

Beau rolled his eyes as cooking steam washed over them. "He better have a damn good excuse." He crushed his beer can.

Willa snickered from behind her hand of cards.

Another half-hour ran off the clock before dinner was ready. Beau looked proudly over the spread on the kitchen island and instructed someone to go check on Andy and Eden. It was Jake who volunteered. He tip-toed into their room and was back in less than a minute.

"They're out like a light," he said. "Those brownies must have hit different."

"You sure they're breathing?" Freddie laughed.

Beau took Delco a plate as we formed a line and served ourselves. We convened at the table, five friends lighter than the night before, and there wasn't much small talk. There was no blessing. There was the chew-

ing of food, the clink and occasional squeal of silver-
ware on good plates. A stray slurp from a glass or a can.
As we ate, snow began to drop in thin, steady shrouds.

Chapter Twenty

"Getting out of here in the morning is gonna be a real pain in the ass," Freddie said. He was peering out the picture window. The falling snow wasn't heavy, but it was consistent, and at this elevation with these temperatures, the ground was almost sure to become a terrain that only a Zamboni could traverse by sunrise.

A few of us were in the kitchen cleaning dishes. It was nine o'clock.

"I hope Mike and Maggie make it back all right," Livy said as she wiped a plate with a dishtowel.

Beau dropped some forks into the dishwasher. "They'll be fine," he said, surprisingly dismissive. Then again, he had consumed a lot of beer. "My truck has four-wheel drive."

"You really think Mike knows how to use four-wheel drive?" Jake asked. He was starting to slur his words. "The dude's NASA smart, but he can barely tie his shoes."

"No," Beau answered. "But Maggie does."

As soon as the dishwasher was off and running,

we convocated at the dinner table like a tipsy tribunal, passing cheeky judgment on one another while the remains of the night wasted away and the free-flowing booze continued to loosen the day's morose grip. The others finished off drink after drink, and I rode the low of my most recent dose. I had snuck into the bathroom for yet another pill right after dinner, and now I was pleasantly drowsy.

Laughter rose and fell over the room like a bedsheet on a clothesline in the middle of a spring breeze, and so did smiles. Smiles so wide they hurt. We did what people inexplicably do when they're having a great time: talk about other great times they've had.

Beau's face was as red as the tomato sauce he'd cooked earlier. "Remember freshman year when our party got busted, and Jake's dumbass climbed the fire escape and went and hid in the dumpster?" He hucked a deep belly laugh.

Everyone else did, too.

Freddie snorted, a signature of his once he started in on the liquor.

The visual of Jake unnecessarily hunkering down in a dumpster full of rotting garbage for an hour— decked out in an expensive pair of jean shorts, no less—was quite the image.

"I didn't get a drinking ticket, did I?" Jake asked, turning up his beer. "Not that night."

"My man was gone," Beau said, snapping his fingers for effect. "I'm surprised we didn't see a repeat of that earlier, to be honest. I could see you thinking about it when that big, fat motherfucker rushed us this morning."

There was a recollective huff in the room.

"I could've gone the rest of this trip without you

117

bringing that up," I told Beau. "That shit's gonna haunt my dreams for the rest of my life."

"You looked like you had control of the situation to me," he replied. He lifted his fist to his mouth and chuckled. "I seen you whip that pocketknife out. Fixin to cut a bitch."

I smiled. "Like that beer can you were getting ready to hurl was much better?"

"Hey, I was just gettin right with the Lord in case He was about to call me home. I got a lot of explainin to do."

Freddie butted in. "She was lucky I wasn't here," he said, air boxing above the table. "I woulda two-pieced her ass back to the Hundred Acre Woods."

"What about the babies?" Willa asked.

His face was as straight as possible. "I woulda spazzed on them, too."

"Says the guy who had to sleep with the lights on after we saw *IT*," Livy said.

We laughed.

Beau went back to regaling us with stories from college, some I had been there for, some I hadn't. My medicine was kicking in now. Everyone moved back and forth from the fridge and coolers in slow motion, drink after drink, joke after joke, stumble after stumble, like in a misty montage played at half-speed. Shots were taken. Beers were shotgunned. A joint was rolled. For the first time in a long time, I got the feeling that everything was going to be all right.

At some point, we migrated to the living room, where Jake and Freddie were having an intense game of *I Bet You Won't*. I circled the furniture and admired the Singer sewing machine. Its oak was well-worn and chipped in places, but it was still stained a chestnut brown and in decent shape compared to some of the models I'd seen over the years. My grandparents had had one just like it in their townhome, and tapping at the treadle was always comforting and nostalgic for me. I did so now with my toes; it see-sawed up and down, grating the airwaves with its screeching song.

Freddie's voice surged from behind it. "I bet you won't eat one of those puzzle pieces," he said to Jake.

Jake, wearing the zombified expression of Franken-stein's monster, picked three pieces away from the corner of the puppy puzzle. Then, without breaking eye contact with Freddie, he shoved them into his mouth and began to chew like a cow on cud.

Half of us laughed, and the other half recoiled in disgust.

"Christ, dude," Freddie said. "I didn't think you were actually gonna do it."

Jake started to swallow, then thought better of it. Instead, his Adam's apple lurched up his throat in a gag. He staved it off, stared straight ahead.

"You gonna puke?" Danielle asked.

"Yes, ma'am," Jake slurred through his half-full mouth. He carefully got up, staggered to the sliding glass door, and disappeared around the corner of the porch, presumably to throw up over the side of the railing.

"What am I gonna do with him?" Danielle asked to no one in particular. She was in a bad way in her own right, sitting at the coffee table with her legs folded and a drink the size of a Big Gulp in her hand. She reached under the table with her free hand and came up with an old Fig Newtons tin. "What a strange thing to have," she said, giggling harder than she should have. She studied the front of the container. "Since 1891? Fig Newtons have been around since 1891? Imagine someone in the

1800s was like, 'You know what we need? Some fig ass cookies.'" She was reduced to hysterics as she opened the tin and removed a small, round black object. "Why are there circles in here?"

"That would be a checker, Danielle," Beau said.

Danielle cackled. Willa and Livy laughed at her side as she continued to fall apart, and the sight of it put a grin on my face. It was shaping up to be a hot mess of a night.

"I love you guys," Danielle said, standing. Sort of. "Bring it in," she beckoned dryly, motioning to all of us.

We locked arms in a wobbly group hug, me, Willa, Livy, Freddie, Beau, and Danielle.

I turned my attention toward Freddie, who, once past a certain threshold of alcohol consumption, became his alter ego, "Weekend Freddie."

"How're you feeling?" I asked him.

"Yes," he simply said.

"Hey!" Danielle blurted, breaking our arms apart. "Delco should be here for this. Let's go get him."

Chapter Twenty-One

When we got downstairs, Delco was still on the sectional sofa in the supine position. His eyes were now closed, and his breaths were on the shallow side. He didn't have much color, but he wasn't ghastly pale, either.

I scratched my chin as I examined him. The flame of the fire was warm on my skin. "I don't know. I still feel like maybe we should get him some help."

"He's good," Beau said. "He's just sleepin it off."

I felt a few of the others nodding. But how was I to trust them? They were three sheets to the wind, even Willa, who was starting to hit me with her trademark tipsy grins. Then again, so was I—in my own way. I didn't like Delco, but I didn't want him to not wake up. Beau reached into the pocket of Delco's jeans carefully, like he was trying to steal a bone from a sleeping dog. He wiggled the big, cumbersome-looking smartphone free and deposited it into his own pocket.

"What are you doing?" I asked.

"I wanna take some selfies," Beau garbled. "He's got Portrait Mode on this thing."

Suddenly, I felt old because I didn't know what that was. We left Delco to recover in his pseudo-coma and gathered at the kitchen table, which was now a smorgasbord of cans, airplane bottles, plastic cups, shot glasses, and cigarette lighters. I didn't even want to think about what the cleanup effort would be like the next morning.

Beau swayed at the end of the table like a drunken king amongst his royal court. "Let's play some music!" he chanted.

"Yeah!" everybody agreed.

"I'm not so sure that's a good idea, Beau," I said. "The sheriff—"

"Fuck the sheriff," Beau barked.

"Fuck Jimmie Wimmens," Danielle concurred.

"Beau," I said.

"What are you, the deputy?"

I frowned.

"I'm just messin with you." Beau laughed, slapping me on the chest with the back of his hand. "Let Johnny Law come knockin. I'm on vacation. Who's got aux?"

"Me," Danielle shouted.

She pecked at her phone with her thumbs. Then a mellow tune began to play, and it chilled my spine. It was "Take Me Home, Country Roads."

Everyone cheered, except for me and Willa. I felt myself flush as they sang the first verse and chorus. It had been the second that was so off on the car ride up, and so I cringed as I waited for it to come. I expected it to be just as eerie as it had been then. But it wasn't. It was John Denver's normal dulcet voice and picturesque words. I breathed a sigh of relief.

By the third chorus, Beau was belligerently hollering "mountain mama" over and over again.

And for some reason, my mind couldn't move on from that bizarre cover from the car. What had the lyrics been? "I was lost once, but by faith was found. Shouted glory, Hallelujah, like…" Like what? I recited the words in my head to the tune of the background instruments: *"I was lost once, but by faith was found. Shouted glory, Hallelujah, like a…like a hound?"*

Like a hound?

Like a hound.

I gasped. It raced before my eyes. The red lights on the side of the Blue Ridge Mountains. The smell of sulfur. The lady in the scorched earth of her front yard. *Have you seen the dog?* What the merchant had said in the General Store. The vision I'd had of the preacher in the First Baptist Church. A numbing terror overcame me like evil over good. It had to have been close to midnight. Where the fuck were Mike and Maggie? Where was Jake? My legs became as weak and watery and loose as cake batter.

Somewhere outside of my head, Beau was saying, "Let's get a selfie."

Livy was saying, "I'm gonna go wake Andy and Eden up," and Weekend Freddie was telling her to leave them be.

We crowded together. Beau snapped a pic and promptly backed out of the app to see what it looked like. His smile waned. We looked at the screen. The backdrop of the kitchen was there in the photo. There was just one problem.

We weren't.

Chapter Twenty-Two

"It's just a glitch," Beau slurred, his eyes locked on the empty room staring back at him from the screen of the phone. "That's all." There was something frantic in his voice. He stabbed at the Home button frenetically, but nothing changed. The song had ended and quiet replaced it. It sounds crazy, but in that moment, I could hear every heartbeat in the room. I'm sure of it.

Then there was a hum like electricity, low at first, but building higher. Higher. Higher still. We whirled around to locate it. In the corner of the living room, the treadle of the Singer sewing machine teeter-tottered up and down, up and down, banging against the floor, metal on wood, and the flywheel spun until it screamed. A form unseen was fabricating something vile. Something possessed.

Willa covered her ears.

Livy's face was all eyes.

I heard an almost inaudible growling noise. The puppies on the coffee table puzzle were snarling and yowling, hot coals where their adorable eyes had been.

They weren't wallowing in laundry anymore, but rather some putrid, inky marsh that matted their once-soft fur. Hellions masking their once-pure odor with unimaginable stink. I shook my head vigorously in the hope that doing so would make them go back to normal. But still they sneered. Their puling was soon overshadowed by a babbling at the end of the table.

In *The Last Supper*, Jesus and his disciples turned their heads toward us, judging, leering, eviscerating. They stood at the table, their robes billowing like villainous capes, chants rising in a cultish ritual. The paint was bleeding.

The overhead lights blinked with a nervous tick.

"What in the most *entire* fuck?" Freddie said.

Beau jumped from one sight to the next. "I specifically told that man no funny shit in the brownies."

"You're not hallucinating, Beau," I replied.

The sewing machine, puzzle, and painting were duking it out for which among them could be the loudest, the most loathsome. They were all equally terrible, reaching for a crescendo, when Andy barreled into the room, eyes crazed, breath erratic. His clothes were speckled with brushstrokes of blood.

"I can't find her," he panted. "I can't fucking find her."

"Hold up, hold up," Freddie said, squaring Andy by the shoulders amidst all the chaos. "What's going on?"

Andy ripped away. "I can't find Eden, man. She's gone. I woke up, and she wasn't there." He held up his hands and examined the blood like it was the first time he was seeing it. His lips trembled. "Oh, fuck. Oh, fuck, oh, fuck, oh fuck!"

"Take it easy, bro," Freddie said.

But then we heard something else. It was a knocking noise, and it was coming from the little laundry room in the corner of the kitchen.

Beau took one look. "Oh, hell no," he said. "Mama didn't raise no dummy."

The rest of us lined up in a formation fit for the Roman legions, me at the lead, and cautiously proceeded toward it. Every step felt like a mile. As we neared the room, I could see that the washing machine was in the rinse cycle, though none of us had started a load. The splatter on its white exterior matched Andy's shirt. A gruesome arrangement of red.

I tip-toed ahead, extending a hand to open it, but Andy bolted past me and threw the lid upward before I got a chance. He wailed, his grief so intense it drowned out what was going on in the next room. The tub was filled to the brim with a brothy, pink stew carrying chunks of what appeared to be regurgitated remains. As they agitated back and forth, a human hand bobbed to the surface of the foul water.

There was a scream, but from whom I don't know. Andy cried out and backpedaled against me with such force that it was a miracle he didn't knock me down. I held onto him for dear life, and he pushed me back into the kitchen against the others.

We hurried into the living room, an unspoken agreement among us: it was time to go.

That's when a bawling song of sorrow escaped the bowels of the house. There was a panicked patter of footfalls that, in an instant, became deliberate and sluggish on creaking steps. Delco crawled up the basement staircase in a contorted spider-walk. He halted on the top step and howled, still on all fours, a liquid the consistency of slobber pouring from his mouth, his eyes, his ears.

We cursed and recoiled in horror, Beau and Danielle falling over the coffee table. I glanced at them and looked back up just in time to see Jake's body burst through the sliding glass door, sending shards of glass glittering to the table and floor. He didn't have a face. A bone bowl of exposed sinuses and bloody, pulped brains now existed where one had been.

Danielle released a blood-curdling scream that seemed like it would never end.

Once it did, our nightmares became Hell on Earth. The beast hurled through the hole created by the shattered sliding glass door and went straight for Delco. It moved so swiftly that I couldn't get a clear look; I just knew that it was a long, black quadruped—maybe as long as nine feet. Maybe longer. There was a halo of vermillion around its head. It bit into Delco's weeping face, and the sound of facial bones breaking and separating echoed across the room.

"Jesus Christ!"

Delco was reduced to a limp, faceless body in a pool of saliva and blood, and the beast turned its attention toward Andy, who was trying to flee with a face wrought in unparalleled fear. It clawed his neck and sent a gout of blood surging toward the wall as he shrieked. Then the beast chomped on his arm, rending it in two. The severed hand and forearm squirmed back and forth on the ground like a tongue hitting the walls of a mouth. As Andy puddled on the floor, the beast hovered over him, and while I couldn't be certain, it looked as though the monster was licking his eyes, lapping at them like a large, thirsty dog might do with water.

It all happened so fast.

The beast's next move seemed like a forgone conclusion, but I still couldn't divert my eyes. For every train wreck, there's a frozen and hypnotized spectator who just can't stop looking, even when they're in the path. That night it was me until Willa tugged at my arm, saved my life. Then we ran like hell.

"Let's get the fuck outta here!"

"Go, go, go!"

We spilled over one another in the hallway and scrambled into the front bedroom, the sound of death falling behind us. We busted through the front door into the snowy, dark mountainscape of the outside world. A world that felt no kinder. I searched my pockets and turned up Willa's keys. We piled into the SUV, and I fired up the engine. We headed down the mountain.

Part 3

Chapter Twenty-Three

Snowflakes clung to the windshield, and the wipers, jacked up to full-speed, ground them into bleary, rainbow-shaped streaks. The SUV's tires slipped on the loose ground like socked feet on hardwood floors as I pushed the accelerator as far as I could without losing control. The surrounding trees beyond the gate, great and cupped inward, held us as their damned little darlings. Mouth of Sheol had become a frozen hellscape from which there seemed to be no deliverance.

"What was that thing?" Livy hollered, a distinct wobble of turmoil in her voice. Danielle's face was buried in her shoulder. She was sobbing uncontrollably and repeating Jake's name over and over. She hadn't even gotten to say goodbye.

Freddie was saying fuck a lot.

"What *was* that thing?" Livy repeated.

"I don't know," Willa said.

"Don't you see?" I snapped, smacking the steering wheel and letting the moment get the best of me. "It was a hellhound!" I could hardly believe it still.

"That's ridiculous, Heath," Willa shouted. "Hell-hounds are cryptids. They're not real."

"I don't know," I laughed. "That seemed pretty fucking real to me. Or am I the only one who saw the humongous black monster eat three people's faces back there?" I glanced at her. "What species of mountain lion grows close to ten fucking feet long without counting the tail? Have you ever heard of any black bears that can make pictures and puzzles come to life?"

"I'm just trying to be logical," she yelled defensively.

"There's nothing logical about this place," I said, a sensation of shame welling up inside of me for having talked to her that way—regardless of the circumstances. It wasn't her fault.

Freddie had been trying to dial 9-1-1, but he wasn't getting any signal. "America's number one network, my ass," he said, spiking his phone to the floorboard. Weekend Freddie had worn off.

"What's your take, Freddie?" I asked. "That thing look like any of the hellhounds you came across on your Google escapades?"

"If it didn't, I'd hate to see what the real one looks like," he said.

A fog sunk its teeth into the path as we made it a mile away. The rear windshield was occluded by gathering snow and darkness. For all we knew, the monster was right on our heels. I motored forward at a crawling speed, but with the lack of visibility and traction, it felt like I was bending corners on a speedway. On a particularly steep decline, I came in too hot. I overcorrected, the steering wheel juddered in my hands, and I nearly spun out. I found my footing just in time to avoid the trees. But nobody panicked. I think we had all realized something at the same time.

"Wait," Freddie said. "Where's Beau?"

We looked at each other, then I glanced in the rear-view, hoping he was somehow in the cargo hold.

"Shit," I said, a feeling of freefall in my stomach.

"Oh my god," Livy gasped. "We have to go back for him, y'all."

"If we do, we're dead," I said, quickly and gravely. "Besides, there's nowhere to turn around."

"No, Livy's right," Willa said. "We can't just leave him."

"We can't go back, Willa. It's too dangerous. You know damn well that Beau would be the first one to tell us to save ourselves."

I could tell she agreed, but that didn't make it any easier. Her mouth began to tremble, and her brown eyes glistened with tears as we came upon the shack where we'd met the questionable old lady the night before. It felt like so long ago—like a scene from a scary movie you saw as a kid or a memory that's so embedded yet so unlocalized that you're never sure it happened at all. The shack's porchlight burned between the two front windows like a parietal eye, stealthy, cold-blooded, and in its luminous reach, vaporous tendrils climbed above the front yard.

A funny notion crossed my mind. *Maybe I should go in there*, I thought. *Maybe I should kick that shitty door in and let that old bat know I found the "dog."* But I didn't. I kept driving. I kept driving until we happened upon a flock of soft shapes, ill-defined in the fog. My hair stood on end until we were right up on it, and I realized it was the goats from up the road. They were quite a ways from their barn, scattered and aimless-looking, maybe half a dozen of them, so still they might as well have been stuffed. I blasted the horn at one of the stragglers that was on the edge of the path just enough to be in my way, and it looked at me with empty, penny-colored eyes. It appeared to be lying down.

"Get the fuck out of the way, goat!" I barked, hammer-fisting the horn again.

The goat bleated but didn't move. As I eased off the brake and rolled forward a few inches, the fog broke, and I could see why it wasn't moving. The legs on its right side were cleaved off and replaced by ragged, bloody stubs. The poor animal rested there in shock, waiting for Death to take it into His arms, swaddle it, and steal the pain and carry it into absolute dark.

"Son of a bitch," I said. "It never ends."

Willa grimaced and turned from her window. I wrung the steering wheel. For the second time in as many days, I had the opportunity to do the decent thing and help a living creature die with dignity. I should have mowed over the goat's neck with three thousand pounds of pressure—some dignity, I know—but I chickened out. Instead, I did my best to maneuver around it and kept squeezing down the mountain. I didn't know if I could take anymore. The adrenaline from the house was wearing off, and so were the desirable side effects of the drugs. I was now only left with the muzziness and the fatigue. I kept waiting for the ride to end—for the restraint bar to be lifted so that I could sprint out of this diabolical amusement park as fast as greased lightning and never look back.

I committed the cardinal sin of thinking it couldn't get much worse. I couldn't have been more wrong.

Chapter Twenty-Four

It was only another minute or two before we came upon another sight that made my heart sink faster than a body with cinder blocks tied to its ankles. Tucked into the trees on the left-hand side of the road was the tailgate of Beau's truck. The lights and engine were killed, and so the old pickup sat there like a getaway car hiding out from the law. The driver's side door was open.

Words eluded me for a moment. Then I remembered what was at stake. "I'm gonna go check it out," I announced.

"Heath, no," Willa replied.

"I've got to. Mike and Maggie might still be in there."

"Want me to go with you?" Freddie asked.

"No," I answered. "Just in case..." I latched onto Willa's eyes. "If anything happens to me—"

"No," she interrupted, shaking her head.

"Listen to me; this is important. If anything happens to me, jump in the driver's seat and get the hell out of here."

She coughed a pitiful little cry that cut me deep.

"Tell me you understand."

"I understand," she said.

"I love you."

"I love you, too."

I unfolded my pocketknife with a shaky hand, breathed in deep, and popped the door open. I hopped out and closed it behind me. Flakes of snow tickled my exposed neck and hands as I tip-toed toward the truck, the knife clenched downward in a stabbing position. It was miserably cold. I exhaled a few heavy breaths, swirling like chalkdust in the night air, and eased toward the cab.

"Maggie? Mike?"

No response came.

I hesitated for another moment, then finding the courage somewhere within, I leaped in front of the open door with the knife primed for action. What I saw made me drop it. They were both upright and buckled into their seats—Maggie the driver, Mike the passenger— but like Jake, they didn't have faces. Their heads were caved-in sacks of slimy, red congealed matter. The blood had already cooled. It was the type of twisted, repulsive shit you only find on the internet. The type of spectacle you'd never get used to, no matter how many times you saw it. I'd been able to hold my dis- gust at the house out of necessity, but I couldn't any longer. There on the mountainside, I whipped my head to the left and puked on the driver's side window.

I lingered long enough afterward to make sure more wasn't coming up. I spat the residual taste from my mouth. Then I picked up my knife and got back in the car.

"They're dead," I said, shutting the door. It was

difficult to grapple with how matter-of-fact that statement was.

A whimper came from the back seat.

"Like the others?" Willa asked.

"Like the others."

"This is not happening," Freddie said.

But it was. And so was something else. I had only thought about reaching toward the gear shift when it showed up. It started below us, then crested the trees and shot along the path like a bullhorn's blast through a tunnel. That distorted, wicked voice. It was gleeful in the most tormenting of ways, those flat lyrics sung with an unapologetic love for damnation.

"What the fuck is that?" Freddie asked.

"Its theme song," I said.

John Denver's imposter carried on: "I was lost once, but by faith was found. Shouted glory, Hallelujah, like a hound. My redeemer come down and rescued me. If you don't repent now, you will never leave."

"Theme song?"

It sounded far-off, but it wasn't. It was amongst us, a crooning specter dangling what remained of our sanity from marionette strings. And it was enjoying every second. I don't think I realized it at the time, but the voice was trying to take *me* home.

"We're gonna die," Livy gulped.

I didn't disagree, but I didn't wait around for it to happen, either. I thrust the SUV into Drive, and we lunged forward, leaving Mike and Maggie in their pick-up truck coffin. The song didn't end until we passed the yellow double-wide with the sign on its shed, and we made it to the end of Mouth of Sheol Road without further incident.

"Where are we going?" Willa asked.

"To the police," I said, turning out onto Yellow Sulfur Springs Road.

"Fuck that shit," Freddie responded. "We need to go to the Feds."

"Maybe he's right," Willa said.

I huffed. "Look, I don't like these guys either, but they're probably all we've got. I'm not fleeing the scene of six dead bodies without notifying someone immediately."

We plunged deeper still into a night the moon had forgotten. The roads were slippery, but they weren't as bad as the mountain trail. Soon, we were on the Aylett Mercer Parkway, a pearly white bullet floating through cold, black space. Alone. To me, nobody was going to be there. To me, nobody was going to believe us. We were a traveling carnival of lost souls.

We passed through residential neighborhoods. There was something forbidding about them—like the houses were wearing demented secrets on their faces— like all the light they'd ever held had been sucked into the void. Our present circumstances gave their baleful yard signs new meaning. But I didn't have time to think about that. I was only braking once we reached the police.

When we got to downtown Blue Brier, it looked as though no one had lived there in a hundred years. There was hardly a light to be seen, and the silence was ubiquitous. But I didn't concern myself with that, either. I came in squealing and parked on the curb outside of the magistrate's office. We exited the SUV, strode past the Confederate statue, its stone face pressed against a bayonet and scowling in the witching hour. We raced for the entrance.

Chapter Twenty-Five

I rammed the crash bar so hard that I thought I was going to knock the door off its hinges, and we poured into the lobby of the Blue Brier Magistrate's Office, out of breath and off-balance. It was a cold room with a high ceiling, blue-gray walls, and laminate wood flooring. There was no furniture, save a desk that was embedded into the wall before us with a thick glass screen and one of those circular speak-thrus that you'd find at any theater box office. On either side was a pair of double doors marked by official-looking white letters. The doors to the left read "Holding." The doors to the right read "Courtroom."

We hurried to the desk. It was quieter than a church during prayer except for a raspy jingle coming through the intercom above. I could barely make out the lyrics: "I've got the joy, joy, joy, joy. Where? Down in my heart. Where? Down in my heart. I've got the joy, joy, joy, joy…"

Failing to find a button or bell of some kind, I began to rap on the glass with a closed fist. Willa joined

139

me.

"Hello!" I hollered.

"Help!" Willa shouted.

It seemed like forever before someone rounded the corner in the area on the other side of the desk. It was a mean old cuss in a heavily starched uniform that matched the color of the walls. He cast a sheaf of papers to the desk and glared at us with a severe underbite like we'd just disturbed him from a good night's sleep.

"Excuse me, sir," I said.

"The hell do y'all want?" he yapped, the swales beneath his eyes deepening with aggravation.

"We need to speak to the sheriff."

He cleared his throat. "You wanna file a report?"

"No, I want to talk to the sheriff."

"You cain't just speak to the sheriff without filin a report."

"Get me the goddamn sheriff!" I roared, slamming my open hand on the glass.

For a moment, the man stared at us, and there was only the music: "I've got the joy, joy, joy, joy. Where? Down in my heart. Where? Down in my heart." He disappeared around the corner.

In no time flat, Sheriff Jimmie Wimmens came strolling through the door with "Holding" written over the top of it, cool as you please. "What seems to be the problem, folks?" he asked, a rictus of mild concern on his face and a sucker stick jutting from the corner of his flat mouth. He now wore a t-shirt that said:

1 cross + 3 nails = 4given

It was so big on him that he practically swam in it.

I swallowed. Finding the words for it was difficult

now that I had to say it out loud.

"Spit it out, son," he said.

"Our friends were attacked. Six of them. Maybe seven. They're all dead."

The sheriff looked at the mean old cuss behind the desk, then back at me. "Six of them? *Dead?* Good heavens, from what?" There was something off-putting and patronizing in his weaselly tone.

"It was some kind of animal," Willa interjected.

"It was a hellhound," I said.

The mean old cuss behind the desk laughed.

Jimmie Wimmens squinted at me like I was his child and had just given a bogus excuse for breaking a lamp in the house. "Son," he said, snapping the sucker out of his mouth. "Have you been drinkin?"

"No, I haven't been drinking."

"Be square with me now. We don't take too kindly to pranks—"

"I'm telling you, *sir*, it was a fucking hellhound. A goddamn, ten-foot long, face-eating demon wolf!"

A sternness overtook the sheriff's face. "Watch your mouth in here. This is a Christian environment."

My nerves reeled. "Watch my mouth?" I scoffed. "How can you be so calm when I'm telling you half our friends are dead?"

"Heath," Willa started.

"No, no, no," I continued. "We came here because we need some help, dammit! What difference does it make what killed them? People are dead. Are you going to do something or not?"

"Hold on. Let's back up a minute," Jimmie Wimmens said, his words conceding a bit. It was his best fatherly impression. The fluorescent fixtures above gleamed on his red sucker. "Now I was up there earlier today. What changed after I left?"

I hammered out each plot point on the pane of glass in front of me. "We had dinner. Then a get-together." I was trying to avoid the word "party" at all costs. "Everything was hunky-dory until we found one of us chopped up in a damn washing machine like people soup."

Jimmie Wimmens nodded along like I was boring him. I might as well have been background music. The mean old cuss yawned.

"Then," I kept on, "this monster, this thing, whatever you wanna call it, busted into the house and killed three of our people. That we know of. Right in front of our eyes. It killed another two on the side of the mountain. We found them on the way here." I didn't think the supernatural piece would help my case much, so I left that part out.

Jimmie Wimmens meditated on it with as much thoughtfulness as you might afford when thinking about what you're going to eat for dinner. "That's *some* tale," he concluded. He petered off like he was going to add something, but he didn't. He just leaned there waiting for us to tell him what we wanted him to do about it.

"That's all you've got to say to us?" I said. "That's some tale? What kind of nuthouse are you running up here? You're the law, Sheriff. Our friends have been murdered. Are you gonna get up off your ass and do something about it or not?"

Jimmie Wimmens bit the sucker off the end of the stick and sighed. "Well, let's just say for a minute that you wasn't pullin my leg. If what you say is true, maybe you should stop and think about what caused it in the first place."

"What?"

"Come on now." The sheriff glared smugly. "Y'all

seem like an educated group. What was you doin when all of this happened?"

None of us answered.

"You was sinnin. And the wages of sin is death."

I felt a catch in my throat. "Say again," I said.

But Jimmie Wimmens kept going. "I mean, look at you, girl," he huffed at Danielle, ogled her up and down. "Them britches are so tight I can see your religion."

Danielle's tear-swollen eyes narrowed in confusion and anguish.

Freddie stepped up beside me. "Don't talk about her like that," he said.

I balled my fist, and for a moment, I really thought I might hit the sheriff. Looking back, I wish I had.

"Easy now," Jimmie Wimmens said, less concessional this time. He checked his wristwatch. "Lemme phone one of the deputies to go up to the house with me. Y'all hold tight." He unlatched a flip phone from the hip of his belt and mashed out some numbers.

"Let's split," Freddie whispered to me. "This motherfucker's crazy."

"I vote that, Heath," Willa said. "Something's not right here. Something hasn't been right here all along."

I heard their pleas, but they didn't register. I was too busy listening to the sheriff. Flip phone pressed to his ear, he had taken to humming something while he presumably waited for the party on the other end of the line. Then he began to half-hum, half-sing—a word here, a word there.

A prickle of fear sizzled at my temples.

Jimmie Wimmens grinned at me, his dentures impossibly white and even, his eyes upside down crescent moons. "I was lost once," he sang, "but by faith was found. Shouted glory, Hallelujah, like a hound. My redeemer come down and rescued me. If you don't repent now, you will never leave."

The notion of dread I'd received many times at the house on Mouth of Sheol Road found me again. "We have to go," I said. "Back to the car. Move."

I grabbed Willa's hand and yanked her toward the door. Freddie, Livy, and Danielle followed, no questions asked, as Sheriff Jimmie Wimmens and the mean old cuss leered at us. We barreled through the door, our footfalls hollow in the snowy night, hoping to find Willa's SUV perched on the curb ahead. But we didn't find the car. Instead, we found a horde of people surrounding the Blue Brier Magistrate's Office. There were over a hundred of them, men and women, each brandishing lanterns that burned an intense red. The more I looked at them, the more one thing became apparent: their blank eyes were reminiscent of the man we'd met in Yadkinville.

Livy screamed.

"Fuck," Freddie stammered.

The flock closed in on us, two familiar faces lingering at the front of it. The general store merchant, still in his apron, gaped at us in a manner suitable for the undead, the red of his lantern staining his face like an emissary to the Prince of Darkness himself. To his right, the lady from the shack on Mouth of Sheol Road plodded toward us. Her planter's coveralls were smeared in dirt—and something else. Something deep, reddish-brown. She was spouting nonsense in an otherworldly tongue. All of them were. Some kind of gurgling, disyllabic babble.

"What do we do?"

Freddie spread his arms out at his sides, shielding

Livy and Danielle. A thin man separated himself from the others, and as he neared, I wound up as much adrenaline as I could muster and punched him in the face. He dropped to the ground almost disinterestedly, and then the General Store merchant was upon me. As he seized me by the collar of my shirt, I had to act fast. I drew my pocketknife, unfolded it, and plunged it deep into his windpipe. I could feel every bit of the blade entering, pushing through skin and connective tissue and cartilage as a geyser of blood erupted from the fleshy gap above his sternum and jetted into my face, hot and metallic-smelling. But he didn't fall. He stared at me, his face an inch away from mine, more blood oozing from his open mouth, into his beard, and onto his apron.

Freddie socked two or three of the attackers in the face. Willa kicked one of them in the balls. But then the rest of the mob swarmed us in a flash. Something detached my hand from the knife, pried my fingers until I could no longer hold on. Something separated my other hand from Willa's hand. There was screaming and jabbering and pandemonium. I heard Willa say my name. Then something fell over my head, swallowed it in darkness, and what little light was left went out of the world.

Chapter Twenty-Six

If anybody tries to tell you they're not afraid of the dark, they're probably full of shit. That's where we spent what had to have been an hour or more—in the bitterly cold, full dark of what felt like a walk-in cooler. It was as if we'd gotten to Hell only to discover it was on the opposite end of the temperature spectrum from what we'd been told all our lives. I couldn't see anyone else, but I could hear their sniffles and coughs and whines. The sounds of their despair. I couldn't see my hands or feet, either, but I could tell that they were bound to something. And what's worse, I was clammy and fitful with the onset of withdrawals. Claustrophobia set in quickly, and I began to wrench and grunt, panic overwhelming me. In the background, that loathsome rendition of "Take Me Home, Country Road" was playing softly through old radio speakers.

"Where the fuck are we?" a voice asked, and I recognized it as Freddie's.

"I don't know," I whimpered. "Is everyone here, at least?"

"I am," Livy said.

"Me, too," Danielle snuffled.

"Me three," Willa added. I almost fell apart at the sound of her voice.

Our conversation echoed in the chamberlike nothingness, and we could feel the burden of each other's terror. It seemed like we were alone, but I couldn't be sure. Anything could have been amongst us. My head throbbed, and I realized we must have been brought there—wherever we were—unconscious.

"Ain't this some shit?" Freddie said. "I knew something wasn't quite right about this. I mean, what kind of sheriff wears a fucking t-shirt?"

"I'm sorry, guys," I said, twitching. "I'm the one who led us here. It's all my fault."

"No, it's not," Willa said.

"Yeah," Livy agreed. "All that matters is that we're still alive."

"Now, if we can just figure out how to get outta here," Freddie added.

Suddenly, there was a laugh from somewhere around us, and it startled us all. "Get outta here?" the voice said, a whisper through the shafts of a pitch-black, pernicious mine. "Ain't that sweet?" It was Sheriff Jimmie Wimmens. I was sure of it.

Seconds later, bags were ripped away from our heads, revealing a dungeon of a room bathed in red light. It took my eyes a moment to adjust. We were lined up, side by side, tied to wooden chairs by baling twine, all of us frazzled and blinking. I was on the very end, spitting distance from a staircase to my left. To my right, Freddie, Danielle, Livy, and Willa were next to me in that order. To the right of Willa, scant moonlight sank through a cracked egress window. Several bays of what looked like foodstuffs and sundries surrounded us, lanterns suspended from them. Jimmie Wimmens stood next to the one closest to me, the mean old cuss from the Blue Brier Magistrate's Office at his side, five cloth sacks in his hand. The rest of the townspeople were nowhere to be found.

"Howdy," the sheriff said with a pleased-as-peaches twang.

"Where did you bring us, you old bastard?" I asked.

"To the bringin place," he responded. "Y'all won't bein very cooperative, so we had to give you a few knocks on the noggin apiece. You understand, I'm sure."

"You sick fuck," Freddie said.

Jimmie Wimmens sighed. "Now I asked y'all politely to watch your mouths back at the station," he said. "Gail, teach this young feller some manners."

The mean old cuss stepped forward and backhanded Freddie in one fell swoop.

Freddie winced. Then he spat at the old man.

"Don't you touch him," Livy said.

Our captors laughed.

Sweat beaded across my forehead like ball head needles in a pincushion, and if I wasn't on the verge of death, you couldn't have convinced me. That was the closest I'd ever felt in my life. My heart palpitated, my skin crawled with DTs, and my gut squirmed at the reality of this confinement. It was tenfold the dreamlike feeling of being in that church as the preacher morphed into that hideous creature. Jesus is coming. Are you ready? Turn from thy wicked ways. Prepare—

"Why are you doing this to us?" Willa asked the

148

sheriff.

"You did this to yourself," Jimmie Wimmens answered.

"To ourselves?"

"'Whosoever shall deny me before men, him will I also deny before my Father which is in Heaven.' You give us no choice with your actions. This evil, flesh-lovin world needs to be cleansed. You're part of it."

"We were just having fun," Willa said. "We weren't hurting anybody. You're tormenting us for no reason."

"We're doin no such thing," Jimmie Wimmens replied. He wore that same fabricated look of concern as he had back at the station. "We're just a community of people doin the Lord's work. The sheep followin the orders of the shepherd, if you will."

"So, you're a fucking cult?" I said.

"We're a discipleship, answerin our Divine callin."

"You're a fucking cult!" I repeated. "A certified band of fucking lunatics!" Then I lost it. I started to thrash, the legs of my chair bouncing and scraping on the ground. I could feel spit and sweat flying from me, the sharp lines of the baling twine chiseling deep into my skin as I tossed and twisted. I carried on until I had moved about half a foot and was nearly out of breath.

"Easy," Jimmie Wimmens said. "All the hootin and hollerin in the world ain't gonna save you now." He unwrapped a sucker, plugged it into his mouth. "The hour of the Lord is nigh."

The sheriff had no more than finished his sentence when the door at the top of the staircase creaked open, a long, drawn-out mewl. A thick draft of sulfur flooded the room, stronger than I'd ever smelled, and the god-awfulest scratching sound fell down the stairs. Like shackles clawing at rotted wood. From the darkness

149

emerged a massive black paw with footlong, sabrelike nails that gleamed even in the choked light. Then there was a lank yet violently sharp foreleg behind it. And another. And then this rustle of contained rage, almost akin to a horse's snort, yet grueling and demonic and full of a primal evil that couldn't be learned, only born with.

"Get ready for the Harrowing," Jimmie Wimmens said, his command seeming to come from someplace else. "Prepare to meet thy God."

There are seldom moments in life, I've found, when you're too afraid to scream. But this was one of them. In a blink, the shadow was upon us, over us, total, like a solar eclipse on an unsuspecting world.

Chapter Twenty-Seven

My eyes were closed when the hot, rank breath rushed over my face, flecks of fetid saliva with it. The odor of rotten eggs singed my nostrils. One of the girls was crying, but I could barely hear her over the snarl of what stood before me. At that moment, I reverted to a childlike state—a time in my life when I thought something wasn't there as long as I didn't see it. But I couldn't lie to myself forever. This wasn't going away. Nothing—not the thought of Pinto nor the muscle memory of Willa's touch—could prevent me from tripping over every rung on the gamut of fear.

When I worked up the nerve to open my eyes, the beast was there, and in some ways, it always had been. I'd never seen anything like it. You'd think a hellhound would be muscular, and while this one *was* deep-chested, it was otherwise gaunt and looked like it had starved. It wore a mangy black coat that spread wickedly over an angular back and toward a long, scaly, serpentine tail. The square face of a dog, the spiraling horns of a ram, and my God, those eyes—two red cinders that looked as though they could burn out at any moment or carry on forever just the same. The front legs were punctuated by tremendous forepaws, but the hind legs were hooved.

"God almighty," Freddie said.

I heard Jimmie Wimmens say, "That's right."

The old lady from Mouth of Sheol Road stood behind the beast, one hand holding a heavy chain that wrapped around its broad neck like a ridiculous leash, the other clutching a hatchet. Her face was bereft of all expression. "Do y'all know what Sheol means?" she questioned, a repeat of what she'd asked the previous night.

I wouldn't have been able to answer, even if I'd wanted to. I was too caught up in those red stars of evil, the eyebrows above them wrinkled into a glare of the worst intentions imaginable. I'd known darkness, but I hadn't known it like this. Collapsing into that merciless gaze was like staring past the threshold of Hell. I could feel my soul melt, run through the cracks of my bones, gather at my feet.

"You're fixin to find out," the lady said, once it was apparent that none of us were going to answer her. She began to speak to the monster in her gibberish, as if ordering it.

The hellhound panted in my face, fumes licking at my skin like flames at dry leaves. I'd later find out that Sheol is the Hebrew name for a place of darkness in which the dead—both the righteous and the sinful—remain forever and ever. Some interpretations say that its residents—the ones who are damned, at least—are punished there, and I reckon that's about right, because looking into the eyes of that hellhound, I'd never been so tortured or terrified. I felt hopeless. Like someone who prays to the Lord, but the Lord won't come.

The hellhound drew nearer, emitting more of its vile stink with every inch it closed. But there was the smell of something else, too. Urine. I felt a radiating warmth in my crotch and realized I had pissed myself. The beast opened its mouth, revealing grotesque, gore-stained fangs and multiple tongues—I couldn't see how many—each ropy and double-pointed. My eyes crossed inward toward them in a tangle of horror as the tongues snaked closer to my face. Then the hellhound proceeded to lick my eyes. My vision washed into a kaleidoscope of painful colors and shapes, and then the rebirth of something buried yet familiar.

The merchant at the general store had been right. The hellhound's kiss was worse than my deepest fear. It was the moment of my life I wished I could change above all others:

It was an unremarkable Saturday afternoon when I bumbled into the bungalow-style house, fresh off a day-drinking session with some buddies. My mother was planted on the living room couch, arms crossed, eyes on the blank television screen. I could tell she was in one of her moods.

"Hey," I said, hoping to pass without consequence.

"Where you been?" she asked.

"With the guys."

"You were drinkin, weren't you?"

I sighed. "Yeah."

"How much did you spend?" she asked, standing to her feet.

The room was otherwise empty, but it had a weight to it. A mausoleum of words that were being reanimated, even though they needed to stay dead. Every time I got the chance to face my problems, I clammed up. It's easier that way. To sew your mouth shut and let your demons whittle you away from the inside until you're bone powder.

"That's none of your business," I said.

"If you've got money to go out boozin, you've got money to pay me rent."

I turned out my pockets and snickered.

"I'm not laughin, Heath," my mother said.

I stuffed my pockets back inside my pants and brooded.

"I think it's time you found another place to live."

"You're gonna kick me out?" I released a breath through my teeth. Even through the numbness, it stung more than I thought it would. I said, "You do what you gotta do," and stormed off toward my room.

"I'll pray for you," she said.

I whipped around and lost control. The dam holding my emotional turmoil broke. "Praying doesn't do shit!" I barked.

That hurt her. She approached me, drained of her color, a frailty of someone twice her age. "What kind of man are you?" she said, taking me by the shirt.

"Let go of me."

"What kind of man are you?" she repeated. "I didn't raise you to be this way!"

"Let go of me!"

I wrested my arms from her, and in doing so, underestimated my own strength. In a blur of emotions, I cast her to the side, and she tripped over my feet. She buckled to the floor, barely still hanging onto my shirt, her face a stone portrait of shock. It froze that way as she stiffened to the flat of her back and began to convulse.

"Mom," I said, crouching next to her in disbelief. I took her head in my hands, but she looked past me, a grayness flooding her cheeks. Then a bloody froth started to pool on her lips. "Mom," I said again, panic taking hold of me like a rip current. Her body relaxed to the point of limpness, and when I palpated her neck, I couldn't feel a pulse. My fingers trembled over the screen of my phone as I dialed 9-1-1. "My mother," I said once someone answered. "I think she's having a heart attack."

The dispatcher tried to get me to stay on the line so that she could relay instructions on how to revive my mother, but I cast the phone to the floor and started CPR from memory of what I'd learned in high school health class. I was no more than four or five compressions in when I felt something crack beneath my hands like a dry stick. It didn't take long for me to put two and two together: I had broken some of her ribs. I paused for a moment, engulfed by dismay. Then I continued to drive my palms into my mother's breastbone, her eyes unchanging, her tight, brittle ribcage giving beneath the skin. Once it was obvious that she was gone, I doubled over and roared into the room, a voice that sounded stolen squeezing through my lungs. In the distance, the caterwaul of ambulance sirens joined my misery.

And then things that hadn't really happened began to materialize in my macabre flashback. My mother slowly ascended into the air, face bending into a smile, contrived and harlequin-begotten. She hovered there pendulously, bones exploding inside her in great blasts of sound. Rapidly, her head started to spin on her shoulders and throw blood onto the walls like a water sprinkler system as she laughed and laughed. Shadows fell again.

Outside of my trance, I writhed. Every pain receptor in my brain was firing off. My insides warped into an excruciating snarl, and my fingers and toes curled upward like the legs of a dead spider as I wailed. I could feel something beginning to leave me.

But then something else latched onto me, initiating a tug of war with the force of evil that was trying to steal me from this world piece by piece. It was a song, as faint and sweet and redemptive as a river hymn, small at first but spreading out. It was Willa's voice, reaching for me in the dark.

"You're not lost, Heath," she said. "You're right here. *We're* right here. Your friends. Me. I'm right here."

I grunted and hollered.

"Find us, Heath."

I shook like a wet animal trying to get itself dry.

"You are more than the sum of your pain," she said. "You are more than the sum of your pain."

I was slipping away.

"I love you, Heath," Willa said. "I love you."

I expected to feel the fatal puncture of teeth sinking into my face, and at that point, I might have welcomed it. Instead, a familiar drawl interrupted whatever spell I was under and pulled me back into the red room with a burst of light. I looked over to find Beau standing beneath the egress window to the right of Willow. I couldn't believe my eyes.

"Hey, you ugly sumbitch," he said thickly, his words still a little slippy as the hellhound lashed its super-canine head furiously toward him.

"Leave my friends alone."

The beast bared its dripping fangs, and in a breath, it was bestrode him. It pinned him against the wall, claws burrowing into his chest as he kicked his feet and flailed his arms. Then its tongues eeled about his face, and he keened like an animal in a slaughterhouse. Our three captors smiled, enraptured by the violence unfolding before them.

I stole a glance at Willa, who was urgently trying to mouth something to me. But I couldn't make out what it was. She leaned forward, and I realized that her hands were free. She must have slipped her wrists through the knot, and now she was working her ankles loose from the chair legs. Jimmie Wimmens and his accomplices were too distracted by the scene of gore before them to notice.

All your life, you hear that desperate times call for desperate measures—that fight or flight survival instincts kick in during do-or-die situations. You take it as truth. I took it as truth. But even I couldn't have predicted what happened next. Willa sprang up from her chair, seized the hatchet from the old lady, and in one clean swing, buried the sharp end into her forehead with a chilling *thwack*. The old lady's sadistic eyes immediately went cross, and she flopped to the floor.

"You little bitch," Jimmie Wimmens spat, moving toward Willa.

At that moment, Freddie rocked forward just enough to gather some momentum, and then he fell back on his chair's legs. He repeated this once, twice, three times more, until the legs shattered on the hard floor beneath him, and he toppled to his backside. He rolled over to his knees, chair legs attached to his calves but otherwise free, and scrambled to his feet. Hands still bound to the chairback behind him, he charged Jimmie Wimmens headfirst like a man shot out of a cannon. Freddie rammed the sheriff at the waistline and took him down. The mean old cuss fell with them.

Willa stood frozen in place, disbelieving of the carnage she'd wrought.

"Willa, the hatchet!" I shouted.

It took both hands and a foot to the chest of the old lady for her to remove the weapon. Then she quickly rounded my chair and knelt behind me. She carefully sawed at the baling twine with the head of the hatchet until I was released.

"Cut Livy and Danielle loose," I said. "Then get the fuck outta here."

A wave of adrenaline replaced my withdrawals. I dove into the pile of Freddie, Jimmie Wimmens, and the deputy, while the sickening sounds of Beau's hellish agony echoed mere feet away. I took the mean old cuss by the throat with my left hand and hammer-fisted him into a bloody pulp with my right, the rage of that moment surging through me like water through a burst pipe. Even without the use of his hands, Freddie mounted Jimmie Wimmens's chest after a brief struggle and head-butted him square on the nose, knocking the sheriff out cold.

I got to my feet, and then I helped Freddie to his, just as Danielle was shaking the twine from her wrists and ankles. The five of us made for the staircase to the left, not knowing where it would lead, looking back only once to make sure nothing was following us. The hellhound, too preoccupied with its victim, continued its demoniacal assault, vermicular shoulder blades turned to us and protruding under its black fur.

As we bounded up the stairs, we heard the crunch of Beau's face separating from the rest of his skull.

Chapter Twenty-Eight

Even in the absence of light, it didn't take us long to figure out where we were. We had been brought to the basement of the general store, and now we were on the same sales floor we'd visited earlier in the day. We huddled together in the middle of an aisle as Willa used the hatchet to sever the bailing twine on Freddie's wrists. We were all shaken by Beau's selflessness and subsequent demise but realized we needed to move if we were going to make it out of there alive.

"Are you all right?" Livy asked me. A surreal question.

"I'm good. Just a little rattled. What're we gonna do, y'all?"

"Whatever it is, it's gotta be fast," Freddie said. "That thing looked like it was almost done with—with Beau."

"Poor Beau," Willa said.

I reached into my pocket, only to find that my phone wasn't there. "Anybody got a phone?" I asked.

Everyone checked.

Willa frowned. "They took mine."

"Mine, too," Danielle said.

Livy nodded.

"Yep," Freddie said.

"All right," I said. "Let's sort through this for a minute. Freddie. You're the expert on these fucking things, how do we beat it?

"I'm not the expert, man. I read a Wikipedia page once."

"Well, what did it say? Did it say that it had any weaknesses?"

Freddie thought hard on it. "If I remember correctly, you can't kill it."

"Great," Willa said.

"Only deter it," Freddie continued.

"With what?" I asked.

He craned his head to the side, remembering. "Devil's shoestring, monkshood, boneyard dirt. Salt." Something clicked in his head. It took us all an extra moment to catch up: we were in a grocery store. There had to be salt somewhere around us.

"Salt?" I questioned. "You're telling me that table salt can ward off a creature from the depths of Hell?"

"You got any better ideas?" Freddie said. "We've gotta try something."

I shrugged, skeptical. It seemed like a longshot at best, but it was better than waiting to get slaughtered, and so we dispersed throughout the store, looking for salt in the dark. In almost no time, Danielle called from a rack toward the front counter. We swarmed her voice and discovered a moonlit shelf of roughly twenty 16-ounce canisters.

"This'll have to do," I said.

We scooped an armful each and looked at one another, the most common cooking ingredient our only weapon against the biggest threat of our lives. At least Willa still had her hatchet. In any other situation, we might have laughed. Then there was a commotion beneath us like a rumbling volcano.

"We've gotta make a run for it," Freddie said.

The sentiment was mutual. We dashed for the front door, but something caught my eye before we got there. It was the sign behind the register:

This Establishment is Protected by God and a Gun.

I circled the counter and crouched down. In plain sight on the top shelf was a Ruger pistol. I grabbed it and wedged it between my belt and lower back. I even took a can of the bear spray and a refillable aerosol container from the counter—just in case—and added them to my stock of salt. We exited the general store into the pervasive shade of night. In the Harrowing of Hell, Jesus may have come down to save people, but we were going to have to go this one alone.

"What about all the people that were out here earlier?" Willa asked. "They're gonna have to show up at some point."

"Let's take it one thing at a time," I said.

We started moving briskly down the abandoned street—as fast as our legs would go without the aid of our arms—without much of a plan for where we were going or what we were going to do once we got there. But our impetuous efforts were short-lived. From behind, a black fury of shape and sound catapulted over us and into our path. The hellhound's paws made indentations in the asphalt as it settled into the road a body length or so ahead of us. It turned around and arched its back. It drank a deep breath, rib bones bulging beneath its scruffy withers, and lobbed a howl that certainly wasn't reminiscent of any earthbound creature I'd ever heard. The deafening wail caromed through the empty streets like a train screeching toward an emergency stop only to plow into an immovable object. The resulting debris forced us backward.

The hellhound set its eyes on us, kiln-red and almost saurian in their pitiless calculation. The chain still attached to its neck, the beast hulked toward us, and reactively, I dropped my salt and reached for the Ruger tucked in my belt. I aimed the pistol and fired a shot into the hellhound's left shoulder. The bullet produced little more than an oily sizzle of smoke that dissipated as quickly as it had appeared, and the hellhound proceeded, unaffected.

"Shit," I said.

The hellhound stalked forward.

I stepped in front of Willa, waiting for the monster to pounce.

Then Freddie acted. He flipped the cap of one of the salt canisters and emptied it onto the ground, forming a sandy circle that cut through the thin layer of snow around us, five feet or so in diameter. Livy replicated this maneuver, doubling up the lines until they were thick.

The hellhound planted a primed forepaw at the edge of the circle and stopped. It dipped its head and sniffed. After several whiffs, the beast became rigid, pinned its triangular ears beneath its horns, and showed its teeth in a violent display, Beau's blood still fresh on their tips. With an offended look on its face, the hellhound backtracked a few paces and sat down on its haunches like a dog waiting for a ball to be thrown.

"Holy shit," Freddie said. "It's actually working."

As far-fetched as it sounded, he was right. The hell-hound shifted into a lion's pose, glaring at us but refusing to come any closer. One move outside of the circle was a death wish. We huddled close together, eyes fixed on the monster as it lay in wait like it had all the time in the world. There was nothing to suggest that it didn't. Claustrophobia came in a stranglehold once again as the buildings closed in and the surrounding darkness cut everything down to size. Several minutes passed before anyone said anything.

Willa spoke up: "What now? We can't stay here forever."

"Yeah," Freddie said. "I doubt that thing's gonna fall asleep."

I racked my brain for a solution, but nothing came. We would have to leave the safety of the circle eventually, and when we did, it would be a bloodbath. Not to mention, it was only a matter of time before the sheriff and his sidekick came looking for us. And then, of course, there was the rest of the town.

Salt was obviously an Achilles heel for the hellhound, but it wasn't enough. I began to run through its other weaknesses again in my head. Devil's shoestring. Monkshood. Boneyard dirt. I looked up, and the answer covered me in goosebumps like an intense episode of déjà vu: I remembered the graveyard on the hill. It couldn't have been more than a quarter of a mile from where we were standing. Frantically, my mind turned toward how we would get there. I glanced at one of the containers of salt I had dropped on the ground. Then at the can of bear spray lying next to it. I picked both of them up, stowed the gun away again.

"Freddie."

"Yeah?"

"You said that boneyard dirt was one of the hell-hound's weaknesses, right?"

"Supposedly."

I unscrewed the nozzle on the can of bear spray and emptied some of its contents outside of the circle. "There's a cemetery about four-hundred meters away on the other side of the buildings behind us. I don't know what we're gonna do when we get there, but we'll figure that part out later."

"That thing'll chase us down in the first ten feet," Willa said.

"You're right," I replied. "But I think I've got an answer for that." I opened the lid on the salt and poured a heaping portion into the refillable aerosol can. Then I popped the nozzle on the bear spray and added it to the salt. "When I tell y'all to break for the graveyard, don't look back," I said, reattaching the top of the re-fillable aerosol can and giving it a hard shake. "I'm gon-na hold it off until we get there."

"All right," Freddie said.

The hellhound's tongues slithered out of its mouth, and it wagged its tail as it marked our every move, our every word. It was patient, cerebral. The pain of not being able to save my mother located me again, fresh and strange like a new monster. My internal demons and external demons coalesced to form the most perfect fear I'd ever felt. It was time to run again. I breathed in, and aiming the can at the beast, I mashed down on the nozzle. A misty swell billowed toward the hellhound, and it reeled backward, half-howling, half-retching.

"Run!" I hollered.

Everybody took off, and I followed them in a back-pedal, blindly spraying the makeshift mixture at the hell-hound. I was able to hold it at bay as it pursued and dodged side to side with jaw-dropping agility. It loped left to right, backward and forward, agitated and vicious-looking in its chase, hurling murderous noises into the night. We rounded the laundromat, the graveyard in sight, when Danielle slipped on the snow and fell to the ground. I stopped in front of her, bearing down on the nozzle. As Freddie came back and helped her up, the hellhound halted and unleashed another one of its unworldly howls.

Its kingdom come, its will be done, on Earth as it is in Hell.

We kept running, the longest quarter-mile of our lives, and at any moment, I just knew that the thing chasing us would break through the curtain of repellant and drag us to a world in which sorrow fell like hot rain. But we made it to the hill of the cemetery. Half-way up, the can of spray in my hand ran dry.

Without a moment to spare, I chucked the can at the hellhound, turned, and sprinted on numb legs. I saw my Willa's face, and I dove for her.

Chapter Twenty-Nine

The snow had begun to let up, but the graveyard was already smattered, and so the moonfall cast it in a waxen glow. I had made it. We stood just inside the burial ground, and the hellhound paced on the outskirts of it, unwilling to cross the invisible line that separated us. The beast snorted droplets of snot from its round nostrils and glowered. Its breaths were bales of soot in the cold silver.

I scanned the surrounding headstones as I caught my wind. Some were quite old, harkening back to the late nineteenth century. Others were so eroded that they couldn't be dated at all. One to the right of where we stood had been freshly dug to accommodate several coffins and was waiting for something to fill it. It didn't take me long to realize that something was supposed to be us. We had moved from the refuge of the circle to a much bigger haven, but we were still stuck. The prospect of escape was looking dimmer and dimmer.

"Anybody got any ideas?" Freddie asked.

Our batteries were drained. We were each some

combination of intoxicated and on the comedown, and we were running for our lives. There was no immediate answer. I sifted through my brain again for anything, and for whatever reason, the first thought that came to mind was my mother's graveside service. I imagined the undertaker in the toils of his industry, winding on his machine and lowering the casket revolution after revolution into the burial vault. I couldn't bring her back. I would never be able to bring her back. But maybe I could save others. The hellhound had stopped its anxious patrol, and now it was lingering just beyond the cemetery border. Its chain lay slightly in the boneyard snow, and its tail was tucked between its legs. Like Pinto whenever he got in trouble.

"That thing is really scared of this place," I said.

"He's not the only one," Livy chimed in.

"What would happen if—" I paused. "No, that's crazy."

"What would happen if what?" Willa asked.

"What would happen if we brought it in?"

"In here with us?" Freddie said. "I see where you're going, but I feel like that's a stretch."

"There's a reason it's staying out there," I argued. "We could hit it with salt and dirt, and then pull it into that empty grave over there."

Freddie thought about that, looked at the deep pit in the ground. "Fuck it," he said.

I think everyone knew the odds we were up against, but there was no more delaying. It was time to live, or it was time to die. It was as simple as that.

"Me and Freddie will throw at it. Willa, Livy, Danielle. Y'all grab the chain as soon as we do. If this works the way I think it might, we'll join you when our hands are freed up."

The girls nodded and drew closer.

"Shouldn't we say a prayer or something?" Danielle asked.

"I think I'm all prayed out," I said. I squeezed Willa's hand. "But I will say this: whatever happens, I'm proud to call y'all my friends."

"Damn right," Livy said.

The others co-signed. We briefly hugged as a group, all of us realizing this could be the end. I didn't want it to be. My soul longed for redemption.

Freddie and I grabbed one handful of earth and poured one handful of salt apiece. The hellhound readied itself, cowing slightly but still daring us to make a move. We didn't leave it wanting. We pelted the beast on its black hide—first with the salt, then with the boneyard dirt—and it roared in stunned vexation. The girls took hold of the chain and began to tug with everything they had. I jumped in the front of the line, and Freddie pulled up the end as the hellhound barrel-rolled onto its back and came kicking, barking, and clawing into the cemetery. It took all five of us to inch it toward the deep grave, and just as it seemed like the beast might regain its footing, it seesawed the lip of the hole and went scraping, plunging to the bottom with a substantial measure of soil and snow.

"Cover it!" I shouted.

We kicked dirt and bottomed out the salt canisters we had left on the hellhound as it wallowed and scratched in its suffering on the floor of the grave. It lofted the god-awfulest dying moans into the ether, the song of a thousand animals in an abattoir march. Had we not known what we were fighting, we might have even felt pity for it. There were two shovels propped against the grave's new, nameless headstone. I grabbed one, and Freddie took the other. We scooped clumps of wet soil from the adjacent mound as Willa, Livy, and Danielle continued to swipe at the ground with their feet until the hellhound's torso was buried. Then the tail. The paws and the snout. The hellhound undulated beneath the weight of the earth until the trench was half full. Then the devil stopped, and a quiet befell the boneyard like a moment of silence for the interred.

We met the ground, exhausted, and peered over the ledge of the grave. The dirt lay still as though it had never been disturbed. I embraced Willa, and the others breathed a sigh of relief.

"We better get a move on in case this thing decides to dig its way out," Livy said.

"That's a good call," I replied.

As we got to our feet, a low chug broke the ghoulish tranquility. Red and blue lights danced from one grave marker to the next, and a boatlike police cruiser came to rest at the foot of the hill.

Chapter Thirty

"For fuck's sake," Danielle said.

I stepped in front of everybody and leveled the handgun as two silhouetted figures got out of the car and ascended the hill. The Ruger hadn't worked on the hellhound, but I was sure it would work on them just fine. Jimmie Wimmens and his deputy entered the cemetery slowly yet carelessly, and that's when I realized that the sheriff had a shotgun pointed at us.

"Don't come any closer," I ordered.

"Y'all oughta be ashamed of yourself," Jimmie Wimmens said. "Causin such a fuss on God's acre. Young people don't have no respect, Gail."

"They really don't."

"You're outnumbered," I said, nodding over my shoulder. "Even if you shoot me, you've gotta deal with them." I looked at the mean old cuss. "And that bumbling idiot isn't even armed."

"Oh, don't you worry, yet," the sheriff retorted, calm as a millpond. "The rest of us'll be showin up directly." He steadied the shotgun. "Plus, I don't even need to aim this thing. There's more than one name on one of these buck shots."

"We buried your hound back there. There's room for more."

"Yep," Jimmie Wimmens said. "I can see that. That's all right, though. He'll rise again."

Our standoff continued for several wordless breaths as a million scenarios ran through my head. Even in the cold, my sweaty palm made the grip of the gun slippery. I didn't trust myself to break the impasse despite my words of warning.

"Say, why don't we come to a truce on this thing?" the sheriff proposed in his condescending way. "This is just a big misunderstandin."

"Misunderstanding, my ass, you old shithead," Willa said. "You tried to kill us."

"No, ma'am," he assured, and in a bizarre turn, he lowered his firearm. He reached into his pocket, drew a sucker. "We asked nothin more of y'all than we would any other old sinner. We simply asked y'all to slough off your filthy skin and be warshed anew. That's all. We asked y'all to submit to your creator as children in the desert, and now we ask you to pray."

I refused to put the gun down. But I failed to capitalize on the opportunity he was gifting me, too.

"Why don't you point that thing somewhere else, son?" the sheriff said. He put the sucker in his mouth and laughed. "We all know you ain't gonna use it. You couldn't even kill that coyote. Hell, you barely put an old store clerk down back there. How you gonna kill me?"

I wondered how he knew about the coyote, but I couldn't concern myself with that right then. He was right, though. I hadn't killed the coyote. I hadn't killed the goat. I was beginning to see that I had killed, but I wasn't a killer.

"Shoot him, Heath," Freddie whispered.

The weight of our seven dead friends came down hard and collected on my shoulders like snow on a tree branch. I wanted to shoot Sheriff Jimmie Wimmens. But I didn't have to. Danielle grabbed the gun from my hand and put a bullet right between his smiling eyes. He dropped like manure, face drawn in a wry and permanent grin, and a ribbon of his blood spritzed the mean old cuss, who stood there dumbly. Then Danielle shot his ass, too.

Chapter Thirty-One

"Sons of bitches," Danielle said, looming over the bodies, all of the effervescence departed from her, smoke coiling along the barrel of the gun in her hand. Willa and Livy approached from either side and comforted their friend.

Jimmie Wimmens lay on his back, happy as a lark. In his mind, death had not been a concern; it had not been an end. He had been expecting a big welcome on the other side no matter the outcome—a "well done, good and faithful servant." He had truly been a madman.

"All right," I mumbled. "All right. I think we might actually have a shot at this thing."

"I keep making that mistake, too," Freddie said.

I gazed off at the police cruiser below. "Wait here with them, Freddie. I'm gonna check out the situation with that car."

I descended the hill to the tank of a sedan parked at the bottom. I flung the door open, plopped down into the driver's seat, and turned the key in the ignition.

After a few groans, the engine sputtered to life, and I could feel an involuntary smile working its way onto my face. It quickly vanished, though, once I realized the odometer needle was sleeping on the E.

"Of course, it is," I said.

"Any luck?" Freddie asked when I returned to the boneyard.

"We're not getting anywhere in that. It's just about empty."

We huddled like a football team, at a crossroads yet again.

"How're we gonna get outta here, guys?" I asked.

"I got nothin," Freddie said, defeated. "I'm tired. I'm half drunk. I wanna go home."

"Beau," Willa said, a spark of life in her brown eyes.

"What's that?"

"Beau. He couldn't have gotten down the mountain that fast on foot. He must've had a car."

She was right. Assuming the townspeople hadn't commandeered whatever Beau was driving, it should have been somewhere near the general store.

"Okay," I said. "What about the rest of the cult?"

Freddie picked up one of the shovels and held it out and upward toward the breaking sky. If I didn't know any better, I'd say he was admiring it. Willa brandished the blood-stained hatchet she'd carried with her since our escape from the general store basement, and Danielle cocked the slide on the Ruger pistol. I got the hint. I took the other shovel and sized it up in my hands.

Livy knelt beside the corpse of Jimmie Wimmens and lifted the double-barrel shotgun, which was more than half the length of her. It looked cartoonish in her arms. She closed one eye and aimed it at a random tomb-stone. "I think I like this thing," she said.

We were gearing up for our run back to town when a dreadful sieving tone sounded behind us. We barely had time to turn and investigate before the hellhound's gigantic paw burst through the grave dirt, sending us backward and shouting. Its claws whipped and whirled like the blooming petals of some peculiar Hellflower. Then the beast's paw sank back into the ground, and it moved no more.

"Go," Freddie said.

Chapter Thirty-Two

We marched down the hill, side by side, five un-
likely survivors pushed to the brink. We trooped onward
in the lightless night, death in our hands, uncharacteristic
retribution on our minds and in our hearts, past the
laundromat, and into downtown Blue Brier. Sure enough,
a mill of people gathered there, more dispersed than
they had been previously, but waiting on us all the same.
Their eyes were portals of empty white light as they
lumbered at us with little urgency, still under the monster's spell. They spoke the language of the old lady. They
spoke the language of the hellhound keeper.

It was the Harrowing.

The sight of them filled me with a fury I hadn't
known before, and hopefully, one I'll never know again.
I stepped toward the first man I saw and jabbed the
spade of the shovel into his face, knocking his jaw-
bone askew. Danielle painted the sky with another man's
brains, and she emptied the clip into the nameless rabble that followed him. Whirling about like a dust devil,
Freddie cut a woman down at the kneecaps and smashed

in a guy's skull with the flat head of his shovel. Bone chips sprinkled the streets like strange confetti. Gore scattered indiscriminately, blood meal in this garden of slaughter.

Willa screamed and slashed with the hatchet, making slants of red from necks and bellies. "I'm sorry," she announced in a pained jabber.

Livy knocked herself in reverse as she fired the shotgun once, twice, again, sending fistfuls of carnage every which way. "Yeah, motherfucker," she said in her small voice.

One by one, they died. No regard for flesh and bone. Blood in the snow. Blood on our arms, our shirts, and faces. Blood of the lamb. And they seemed indifferent to it all. We carved out a path of destruction all the way to the general store, splits and crashes and grunts, ours and theirs, filling the night. Once we were through the crowd, and only stragglers still chased us, we circled the general store and found what we were searching for: the car Beau had driven down the mountain was still parked there. Andy's Mercedes. We rushed to it, me and Freddie dropping our shovels, and hopped in. The keys were still in the ignition, and if only for a moment, I found myself wondering if it was that easy.

"Beau, you beautiful sonofabitch," I said, starting the car.

"Hurry!" I heard from the back seat.

I threw the car into drive and peeled out, catching glimpses of the remaining cult members in the rearview mirror. But there was something else, too: my face. My cheeks were coarse and blood-streaked with a surreal war paint. My eyes were new and listless. A piece of me had been a casualty of all the madness behind me, and sooner or later, I'd have to figure out which part that was.

Willa vomited in the floorboard of the passenger seat and gasped, "I'm sorry." Just as she had to the people she killed.

No one was going to judge her.

We sped off eastward, kicking blankets of white powder through the otherwise empty streets in our wake. In minutes, Blue Brier would be a memory, a bad dreamscape that only time could isolate. I tried to commit none of it to my mind—the drugstore, the car shop, the gas station with the off-brand pizza restaurant inside of it—but that's not how trauma works. Trauma has a way of sticking with you. I guess I know that as well as anyone.

We booked it toward the interstate, the Alleghenies and the Monongahela National Forest surrounding us. We passed the industrial plant into the civilization outside of Blue Brier, and I began to think about where I should stop. We had more than half a tank of gas, so I decided to put more distance between us and that piece of pandemonium. "Almost Heaven" had been almost Hell.

We crossed the Virginia state line. Then we heard it again. The hellhound's fey scream came avalanching down the mountain, its longest and most gut-wrenching rendition yet. Was it a farewell or a promise? Danielle covered her ears and shoved her head between her knees. The others ducked and looked back. I thought every hair on my body might stand on end for all time.

We weren't even five miles into the state when Freddie hollered, "Look!"

The roadside building's sign said:

Virginia State Police

I barely applied the brakes as I skated into the parking lot. It was only right, given my previous disdain for Virginia, that its state police should be the ones to save the day.

The next few minutes were a blur. They came in short bursts of dreamlike memory. We practically fell out of the car and into the building. The woman at the desk there had no idea what to make of us as we filed in, bloody and enervated like the victims of a natural disaster.

Another man soon accompanied the woman, and he appeared just as perplexed as her—unsure of whether to keep staring or ask us what the hell happened.

I opened my mouth to tell them, but only a gasp would come. The violence-fueling adrenaline forsook me.

I cried.

Willa cried, too.

We all cried.

EPILOGUE

As the sun came up, and we were somewhere in the middle of our six hours of testimony apiece, state and federal agents descended upon Blue Brier, West Virginia. I couldn't begin to fathom what they'd think about what was waiting there for them.

In an interrogation room at the Virginia State Police station, I held nothing back. After a doctor checked me out, I bent the ear of a slack-jawed woman in a pant-suit for what felt like an eternity. She tried to jot notes at first, but after a little while, she deferred to her recorder. That was probably best. I told her about the man in the Bojangles parking lot. "Take Me Home, Country Roads." The lady in the dark. The general store. Jimmie Wimmens. The bears. The dog. The cult. The two-dozen-or-so slain bodies. Mike and Maggie. Andy and Eden. Delco. Jake. Beau.

She considered me like one might approach an ex-traterrestrial visitor: with a calm yet obvious skepticism. In a way, I don't blame her. Once I was tapped for words, she escorted me to a hallway bench where the gravity of the situation was slowly catching up to me. The events were still in the front of mind, but something told me that as the days and weeks and years went on, those memories would mold like a flood-damaged house and become even more toxic. Time is funny like that.

Minutes later, Freddie emerged from another door and joined me. He looked like a stranger.

"Have you seen the girls?" I asked. I wanted to see Willa, and I'm sure he wanted to see Livy.

"Nah."

"Did your interviewer ask you a lot of questions?"

"Not really. Just let me tell it."

"Mine, too."

We talked without looking at one another. As we spoke, more than one hundred people were being taken in for questioning elsewhere. The world was discovering what we already knew. I thought.

"What do you think's gonna happen now?" I asked.

"I don't know," he said. "We live, I guess."

I reckoned that was right. We sat in silence with our heads against the wall for an immeasurable amount of time before either of us said anything else.

"You know," Freddie started. "This would make for a hell of a book." He glanced at me for the first time since we'd made it to safety. "But I ain't gonna be the one who writes it."

I nodded. There was one thing I couldn't get out of my mind: whatever ritual existed between the hellhound and the townspeople, however many times they had carried it out, Jimmie Wimmens had referred to it as the Harrowing. But it was different from what Freddie had told us about. There was nothing Christ-like about it. I guess, to them, the Harrowing wasn't saving people from Hell. It was *sending* them there.

"Mister Marion," the agent in the pantsuit called from ahead. She beckoned me back.

"See you on the other side," I said to Freddie.

We sat in the interrogation room, and she took a breath.

"Agents have been on the scene for several hours now," she said. "They haven't found any bodies."

"That's impossible," I responded, something like a laugh tripping up my words.

She didn't find anything funny about that.

"Blood," I said. "What about blood? The walls and floors of the house alone probably look like a huge fucking Rorschach with red ink."

"They're going to need one of you to go back out there with them tomorrow."

"Out *there*?" I asked.

"Blue Brier."

I assessed the stains on my clothes. Felt the emptiness in my chest. A twinge of fright squirmed across my skin. "Y'all don't believe us, do you?"

She didn't say whether they did or didn't. The thought of returning to that place was enough to send me into a conniption, but they needed one of us to go back out there with them. It only felt right that it was me.

* * *

On Tuesday, I departed the station in the back of a state police car, a change of clothes the only bright spot of the morning. The other survivors had been reunited with their families—albeit not allowed to leave the commonwealth of Virginia—and the loved ones of those who hadn't made it were notified, too. I didn't envy anyone who was around for that part. They were still classified as missing at that point, but anyone who had been there knew the truth.

As we traveled along North I-81, the officer in the driver seat tried to make small talk. "Whereabouts in North Carolina are you from?" he asked. He had a voice that was much older than his face would imply.

"We live in the Triangle," I said.

He glanced in the rearview. "The Triangle? That some kind of borough or somethin?"

"It's just a nickname for a few places that make up a greater area. Durham. Raleigh. Chapel Hill."

"Hmm," he responded with what sounded like genuine interest. "I got me a older brother in law enforcement out toward Beechum. You know anything about that neck of the woods?"

"Can't say that I do."

"Ain't a man of many words, are you?"

"Not especially," I said. "Actually, would you mind if we didn't talk at all until we got there?"

"Suit yourself," he replied. For maybe a minute, there was only the easy bowling of tires on the road. "I'm gonna say one more thing, though. Then I'll shut my trap. You look like you been through it like a pig rolls through shit. Not happy like one, but you catch my drift. Someone did evil on you, or maybe someone provoked you to do evil on them. But you should know that we ain't all a bunch of podunk degenerates out here. Some give a bad name to the rest of us, is all. You can do with that what you will."

That was fair, but I couldn't admit it at the time. Instead, I appraised the mountains, their magic no longer enchanting to me; instead, they had become something to dread. The day was shaping up to be clear, but there was still a gray hue that filled the land with a forlornness; it echoed my depleted mental state. The chemical plant came and went, and so did the curvy stretch of road as we entered West Virginia and sliced through Monongahela National Forest.

I could feel my blood pressure rise as we rolled into downtown Blue Brier. There were maybe a dozen squad cars and unmarked government vehicles combined, and probably just as many men and women in suits. There was still some snow on the ground. But there were no bodies. The officer in the driver's seat threw up a customary wave at an official in the street, and we proceeded past all of Blue Brier's quirks and haunts. A particular weirdness befell me when we drove by the magistrate's office. The Confederate statue on the lawn there seemed to hover over us, following the car in a way that the eyes of people in pictures do. It was forged in a saturated blue, but with a green patina. Hairless and androgynous. I know it sounds impossible, but it looked like Jimmie Wimmens.

The houses on the perimeter mocked me in their gothic expressions, and so did their fundamentalist signs. Jesus is coming. Are you ready? Turn from thy wicked ways. I wanted to personally feed each of them through a wood chipper. We took the General Aylett Mercer Memorial Parkway to Yellow Sulfur Springs. Then the officer turned on to Mouth of Sheol Road, the entryway to Hell on Earth. Within minutes, we were at the first house—the yellow double-wide with the foundering shed.

A handful of cars were there, and agents were poking around the premises. The officer exited first and then let me out of the back. He shook hands with a smug, long-legged man in a designer suit and shoes. They considered me as they spoke several feet away, but I couldn't make out what they were saying. I cast my eyes upon the shed.

"Is there anything we should be looking for here, fella?" the long-legged man asked me after a moment.

But I wasn't paying attention. I was too preoccupied with the sign on the shed.

PREPARE TO MEET THY GOD

"The agent asked you a question, sir," the officer said.

I wandered away as if under hypnosis and momentarily blacked out. When I came to, I was directly in front of the sign. Its letters were clumsy and childlike, but to me, they were no different than blood-spill. I stared at them until they spun a maelstrom of evil that was given a plain-speaking voice. It was liquidy and infinite, an expression of ancient villainy. Violence was summoned from me yet again, and I went apeshit on that white canvas. I could feel all shapes of obscenities flying from me—like a colony of bats in a dark tunnel—as I ripped the sign from the shed and attempted to tear it into pieces with my bare hands. Make shrapnel of it like it had made of us. It took five officers and agents to restrain me.

"Easy now," one of them ordered as I sprawled onto the cold ground. "We don't wanna have to cuff you."

At that point, I didn't care. I was spent, but they hardly allowed me a full minute before imploring me to carry on.

* * *

We trekked up to the fork in the road, an officer leading the way with a bloodhound and a German shepherd on either side of him. That's when I noticed that the truck Mike and Maggie had been in was gone.

"There's supposed to be a truck there," I said. "That's where I found two of our friends dead."

The long-legged agent scribbled something in his leather book.

We could smell the old lady's house—or what was left of it—long before we could see it. The derelict building had been razed to the ground, and now, only smoldering cinders remained, casting wobbly air into the morning like a summer heatwave. The earth around the pyre was clearly disturbed, and so the dogs went to sniffing at it, noses an inch away from the soil at best. It wasn't long before they began whining and pawing.

"Good boys, Axel, Ranger," a plainclothes officer said. He distributed shovels, and a team of men commenced to digging at the flowerbed that had no flowers. As they progressed, an unimaginable smell lifted into the air and joined the tang of burning wood. The team couldn't have been more than three feet down when several of them lurched backward in disgust.

The plainclothes officer removed a handkerchief from his breast pocket and held it to his nose. "I think we got somethin here, y'all," he hollered. He reached the other gloved hand into the spaded ground and came back bearing what looked like a pale, cylindrical rag with a red-frayed end. Only upon closer examination did I realize that it was a severed human arm.

* * *

The excavation of the flowerbed revealed a mass grave there on the mountainside. Investigators uncovered viscera and body parts and gristly bones, some of which belonged to our friends, some of which belonged to our assailants. All told, there were an estimated thirty-three deceased once things were pieced back together.

But there were no heads. Without them, there were no distinct bite patterns, and the coroner couldn't confirm the role of a cryptic beast or even postulate that what we'd seen had actually been some kind of great wolf or mountain cat. To the people who mattered, the hellhound had been a phantom born from the minds of distraught victims. Nothing more.

A newspaper article later summed it up:

At least 97 individuals were charged Tuesday with conspiracy in relation to last month's Blue Brier killings. Authorities said that former sheriff, James P. Wimmens, now deceased, orchestrated the murders of seven out-of-state visitors in a cultish crime reminiscent of the infamous Waco and Jonestown massacres. Of the persons detained, none have been tied directly to the carnage. The investigation is ongoing, according to the West Virginia State Attorney's Office.

In the aftermath, all five of us turned down interviews from virtually every major news outlet in existence. There were few answers to the senseless and impossible havoc. I wish I could tell you that the cult had a cool, catchy name—The Order of the Helldog, The Saints of Sheol—but it didn't. Sometimes evil doesn't have a profound or intricate rhyme or reason. Sometimes evil is bare and meaningless and ignorant and brutish.

* * *

This is the last time I'm going to talk about it. The inquiry into the event cleared us of any wrongdoing. It was the second time in my life that I'd been cleared of blame. My mother's autopsy had exonerated me in her death years before (she'd been the victim of a fatal pulmonary embolism). But in both situations, the survivor's guilt remained.

We all got together one more time for the legal proceedings. We even laughed, something many of us never thought we'd do again.

"Can you imagine Beau's drunk ass escaping the hellhound, hiding in the woods, then driving down the mountain shitfaced to save us?" Freddie said.

Mostly, we just sat in silence, traumatized, grateful, forever changed.

Freddie and Livy moved to California after that. I guess they wanted to put as much distance between themselves and West Virginia as possible. Danielle took a break from grad school to focus on coming to terms with life without Jake. As for me, with each passing day, I think about how things might have turned out had we only known an inkling of what was to come.

Why didn't we just turn around to begin with? The omens were all over the place. They might as well have been displayed on a flashing neon sign.

But all that is pointless, isn't it? I can't change what happened. I can only hope to salvage the bones. I don't necessarily think that everyone needs a traumatizing experience to turn their life around. Those experiences certainly *do* put things into perspective, though.

This process has been about finding purpose, peace, meaning, and forgiveness. Maybe I'll go to church again someday. Probably I won't. I don't know that I found God, but maybe I found light all the same. I've sought therapy. My relationship with Willa is stronger than ever. I've got the ring in my pocket as we speak. I'm just waiting for the right time.

Even nearly a year later, though, questions still find me in the most random corners of night. Delco had encountered that hellhound out there in the dark and survived because he had known real pain before it. But then it came back and got him. Isn't that what the general store merchant had said? That it didn't matter if you got away because it would come back and get you eventually?

And if what we saw dart across the road in Yadkinville had, in fact, been the hellhound, what's stopping it from coming for me in the end? After all, Blue Brier is roughly two hundred miles away from Yadkinville. What's a hundred more?

I never believed in Hell. For me, it didn't make much sense to suffer your whole life only to suffer some more when it was all over. Even now, I think that Hell is something you create for yourself. Or something someone else creates for you. I've been through a little bit of both, I reckon. But still, I can't help but wonder about the hellhound's origins. It had come from *somewhere*. I can only imagine that it returned there once it rended its colossal paw through the salt of the earth.

* * *

"Pinto's at the door," Willa calls from the bedroom.

"Well, take him out," I holler back, situating the last dinner plate onto the dish rack.

"I took him out last time."

I heave a sigh into the townhouse and grin. Somewhere, Pinto is whining. "Hold on, you little goofball," I say as I dry my hands.

When I go into the master bedroom, Willa has already nested in the bedsheets. The comforter is bunched around her, and she looks snug as a bug. She turns her head, eyes sheeny and brown like a riverbed, and regards me with love, wonder, gratitude—like it's the last time she'll ever see me. It's a habit we've both picked up since everything happened.

I ease forward and kiss her on the forehead. "I'll be right back," I say.

At the door, Pinto's backside is wiggling so hard I think he might fall down. He wears a smile of pain. I open the front door, and he goes capering into the front yard. The night is an endless blue.

"Go potty," I say to the dog.

He does. As he prances back to me, proud of what he's done, my attention diverts to the fading horizon. My blood cools. Two red jewels of light hover there like distant UFOs, bright but murky. As if they've been submerged in dark water. I close my eyes, and the smell of sulfur floods my nostrils until I can taste it. Maybe it's real. Maybe it's a memory. Perhaps it's both.

Grief is a monster unto itself.

Pinto is barking and wagging his tail to get back into the house when I finally work up the courage to face the world again. The lights are gone. So is the smell. Hellfire extinguished in an instant, translucent ghosts rising in its stead. A baptism by smoke. It's over for me now, but I'm sure those red eyes will follow me for all the days of my life.

ABOUT THE AUTHOR

Matt Starr is a dog dad from a town in North Carolina that was once considered the textile capital of the world. His work has been featured in Barren Magazine, Empty House Press, The Daily Drunk, Schuylkill Valley Journal, and The Dead Mule School of Southern Literature, where he won the inaugural flash fiction competition award. Matt's debut novella, Hell, or High Water, was published by Main Street Rag in 2018.

And check out these other novellas from
Grinning Skull Press

There's no place quite like Cofton Grange. Set in twelve-hundred acres of hills and woodland, it is a playground for the wealthy where, for the right price, every desire is made a reality.

Tonight is special; a group of hunters have bought into the most exclusive contest, the opportunity to track and kill a fantastic and terrifying creature not of this Earth. The stakes are high, each competitor determined to claim the kudos that will come from taking down their incredible prey.

But as the moon rises and the pursuit begins, each hunter is about to find out that sometimes there are fiercer things than the competition.

Tooth and Claw—The hunt is on!

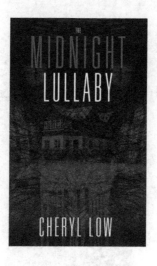

Everybody has secrets…

For years, Benedict Lyon has been living a lie. Not even his family knows the truth he's been keeping from the world. Only Emmeline knows his secret—and she's dead.

…some are darker than others…

When the matriarch of the Lyon family passes away, Benedict is summoned home for the funeral. Emmeline urges Benedict not to go, certain that if he returns to that house, neither one of them will escape.

…but are they worth dying for?

Their presence in the family home causes the spirit of Gloria Lyon to become restless, and as the remaining members of the Lyon family attempt to put their mother to rest, long buried secrets, some deadlier than others, are unearthed. Who will survive…

The Midnight Lullaby

It all started with the sibilant, unintelligible whispering and the movement of shadows within shadows. For Dennis Parkes, it was a sign of his worsening mental health. That is, until the day it spoke clearly and told him what it wanted.

Elsewhere in town, two amateur ghost hunters unearth what is believed to be *Gjallarbru*, a mythological bridge that connects the worlds of the living and the dead.

The dead are looking to cross over, as is the demon guardian, a guardian that has a craving for human flesh. As the veil between worlds weakens and darkness spreads over Ottmor Wood and the surrounding area, it's up to a group of friends to save their town, but are they enough? They have to be—because if they fail, the darkness will continue to spread, devouring everything in its path until there's nothing left to consume.

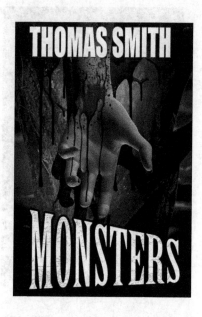

"I killed my parents when I was thirteen years old."

And now, with the murder of Missy Blake twenty-two years later, it's time for Jack Greene to finish what he started.

When the co-ed's mutilated body is found, the police are clueless, but Jack knows what killed the pretty college student; he's been hunting it for years. The hunt has been going on for too long, though, and Jack wants to end it, but he can't do it alone. The local police aren't equipped to handle the monster in their midst, so Jack recruits Major Kelly Langston, and together they set out to rid the world of this murdering creature once and for all.

CPSIA information can be obtained
at www.ICGtesting.com
Printed in the USA
LVHW080315251020
669609LV00003B/95

9 781947 227545